Jill Marshall moved from the United Kingdom to New Zealand, along with her small daughter and her even smaller mad dog. Her childhood ambition was to become an author, so in 2001 Jill gave up her career at a huge international company to concentrate on writing for children. When not working, writing and being a mum, Jill plays guitar, takes singing lessons and is learning to play the drum kit she has set up in the garage. One day she might even sing in a band again . . .

Also by Jill Marshall

Doghead

Jane Blonde, Sensational Spylet*

Jane Blonde Spies Trouble

Jane Blonde, Twice the Spylet

Jane Blonde, Spylet on Ice

Jane Blonde, Goldenspy

Jane Blonde, Spy in the Sky

Jane Blonde, Spylets Are Forever

* Also available in audio

JILL MARSHALL

MACMILLAN CHILDREN'S BOOKS

First published 2010 by Macmillan Children's Books
a division of Macmillan Publishers Limited
20 New Wharf Road, London N1 9RR
Basingstoke and Oxford
Associated companies throughout the world
www.panmacmillan.com

ISBN 978-0-330-45154-3

1 3 5 7 9 8 6 4 2

A CIP catalogue record for this book is available from
the British Library.

Typeset by Ellipsis Books Limited, Glasgow
Printed and bound in the UK by CPI Mackays, Chatham ME5 8TD

For my brave boy fans.
Thanks for daring . . .

1

Jack Bootle-Cadogan moved his home-made Cluedo piece across the board towards his opponent and grinned triumphantly. 'I've guessed it. Wormwood Moonshiner, in the library, with the bicycle pump.'

'Oh, so you think that the beetle boy *inflated* Miss Scarlett to death,' said Albie Cornthwaite with a sniff.

Jack scratched his ear, which was black and hairy and pointed up at the crypt ceiling, and thought for a moment. 'Bashed her over the head with it?'

'I've got it,' said Albie. He twiddled the corner of his little moustache, disguising a tiny smile with his long, nimble fingers. 'He blew into it and used the pump to direct his evil breath straight into her face.'

Jack gagged. 'That would do it. OK, you win. Time to go.'

They cleared the Cluedo board off the top of Granny Dazzle's tomb, and packed it away beneath the altar with the Scrabble, the Egyptian game of Senet, Battle-ships, and a pair of Nintendo DSi's, all the time playing their favourite game of all: Would You Rather.

Jack began. 'Would you rather . . . be breathed over by Wormwood Moonshiner or kissed by Minty West?'

'Oh, Moonshiner breath, without a doubt. Minty is far more scary,' said Albie.

'Same.' Jack curled his lip at the thought, display-ing a magnificent set of pointy teeth.

Then it was Albie's turn: 'Would you rather . . . be stabbed in the head or the chest?'

'Well, seeing as how I suspect I'm immortal, I wouldn't worry about either too much,' said Jack. 'You?'

'Head. It's so hard it would probably break the blade.'

Jack laughed. 'True. So would you rather . . . ?'

On they went as they picked up the camping stools they'd been sitting on at either end of the sarcophagus and made sure that the candles were snuffed out, all except for one or two at the door to welcome any stray souls into the crypt. 'All straight,' said Jack, interrupting Albie's tasty 'would you rather' about eating scarab beetles or sheep's eyeballs. 'Eyeballs,' he added quickly. He'd had some unpleasant experiences with beetles, and given the size of some of the ones he'd come across, he imagined a slimy eyeball would be much easier to swallow.

It had been a quiet night, which was why they'd resorted to playing with their home-made Cluedo set, where a flat cardboard version of Jack's ancestral home, Lowmount Hall, was populated by random characters from their past and present (Ozzy, Ice, Granny Dazzle, Gouldian Finch, to name but a few). Murders were committed with everyday utensils – everyday to them, at least. The bicycle pump might be common enough to most, but not many people would use a staff with the head of a snake very often, or a long iron hook designed for drawing brains through nostrils.

But then most people were not involved with the business of death. Ever since Jack had discovered that his family had been cursed when his great-grandfather Lord Jay found the resting place of the Egyptian god Osiris, he had been busy most nights, dealing with death. In the family crypt he would transform into the dog-headed God of the dead, Anubis, and with the assistance of his undertaker friend, Albie Cornthwaite, he would make sure the souls of the dead people in the graveyard next door made it safely to the afterlife. His first time had been a bit of an experiment, using his new-found powers and a few bits and pieces from the family museum (which was really just a room full of artefacts from his intrepid great-grandfather's expeditions) to transport the ghost of his great-grandmother Granny Dazzle from the mortal plane to the afterlife. When that seemed to go well, he and Albie got started on the rest of the ghosts who hung around the crypt clamouring for their help.

Now that they seemed to have got through the majority of the graveyard, Jack was really quite sad. He'd come to enjoy this night-time banter with Albie, especially as his friend rarely spoke outside the crypt. Albie had been his great-grandfather's assistant and the curse extended to him too: when he was outside the crypt he was transformed into Bone, the ancient albino manservant who was bound to mutely serve the Bootle-Cadogans for eternity.

'Ready to go?' he said softly. Bone much preferred being Albie too, with all his memories – and his speech – restored, so he was always a bit low when dawn and ordinary life loomed.

Albie took a last glance around the crypt, the candlelight dancing off his neat round spectacles and lightly oiled dark hair. 'No,' he said glumly.

'Hey, you think you've got problems? I've got basketball with Minty in a couple of hours,' said Jack. 'Would you rather . . . be Bone for a day or play basketball with Miss "I'm so great I'm an Egyptian goddess with a hawk on my head"?' Jack wasn't the only Egyptian god at his school – there was also Minty (otherwise known as Amentet, whose job was to greet the dead).

But his friend didn't answer, and Jack turned round to find the dapper young man transformed back into the skeletal old valet who had been in his life forever. Jack's own face had shrunk back from its long-nosed, canine, hairy state into an ordinary normal boy's face . . . as ordinary as a kid could be who would one day become Lord Bootle-Cadogan.

'There you are, you old geezer,' he said cheerfully.

Bone quirked a whiskery white eyebrow at him with an expression that said, 'Get you back for that later,' and strode out along the tunnel. After a few minutes of loping along with Jack close behind, he pushed open the door to the Lowmount Hall museum, with its handle in the middle of an Eye of Horus like a knobbly pupil, and they both entered the dusty room.

Ignoring the two figures perched side by side on a long camp bed that had once belonged to his adventurous great-grandfather, Lord Jay, Jack replaced his camp stool in the tent display scene and took Bone's off him to do the same. The museum had become an important part of the tours that helped his parents pay for the monumental upkeep of the hall and its estate, and he had to make sure the display looked the same as always or it would throw off the commentary given by the village ladies who acted as guides.

As Bone headed off to start his breakfast duties Jack turned to the couple on the camp bed. 'Now, Ozzy'n'Ice, Ice'n'Ozzy,' he said to the green-skinned young man with the crook and the flail folded across his chest, and the pale, dark-haired, blue-eyed girl at his side, 'remember you can't stay there on the camp bed. Doris and Mary will have heart attacks if they catch you there, and I'm not on duty at the moment to pass them through to the Field of Rushes if they snuff it. Either get out of the museum for the day, or get in the tent and make like statues.'

'We will be statues today, Jack,' said Ozzy.

'Statues we will be,' agreed Ice, shivering a little.

Jack grinned. 'Statues don't shiver, Ice.'

The piercing blue eyes focused directly on him, and suddenly Ice was not the only one who appeared to be chilled to the core. 'No, but goddesses who are a little afraid do shiver.'

'Shiver they do,' said Ozzy with a nod, eyes darting left and right.

'What are you afraid of?' They were gods, after all – their full names were Isis and Osiris – so surely there wasn't much that could bother them. Mary the guide could be a bit irritating, it was true, and sometimes Doris clacked her teeth in and out in a way that made Jack's stomach turn . . . but this sounded more serious.

'Something is not right,' said Ice, cocking her head as if listening to far-off voices. 'My sisters are unhappy.'

'Unhappy they are,' said Ozzy softly. 'The sisters whisper when something is afoot. They are whispering now.'

Jack held up his finger before Ice could parrot, 'Whispering now they are.' 'So . . . any idea what they're whispering about?'

Ice and Ozzy looked at each other, and Jack's heart sank. 'Not him again?'

He thought he'd got rid of him: Seth, the evil hog-headed Egyptian god who had murdered Osiris because he was jealous of the fact that he was king. Then he had him chopped into fourteen pieces and sent each piece far out across the world, where they could never be found. He hadn't reckoned on Osiris's sister-wife Isis, however, who tracked down all the parts of Osiris except the crown of his head and put him back together again, so he could become God of the Underworld. Then four thousand years later, when Jack's great-grandfather Lord Jay and the young Albert Cornthwaite discovered Ozzy's sarcophagus in a pyramid in Luxor, the furious Seth had risen and cursed both their families. It was pretty complicated, but that was basically how Jack had become Anubis (Doghead to his friends), and why he'd had to face down Seth, who had reappeared in the form of schoolboy Gouldian Finch.

'Is he back?'

Ice shook her head. 'It is confusing. My sisters show me this . . .'

She trailed a finger through the air and icy patterns formed like the vapour trail of a fighter jet. She had drawn a perfect ring with a dot in the middle.

'Isn't that the Eye of Horus?' Jack looked back at the museum door on which the kohl eye was painted. Already he could see his mistake – the pattern Ice had drawn was just the middle of the eye, the cornea and pupil.

'No, it is Ra,' said Ozzy.

'Ra it is.'

'And is that bad?' said Jack.

Ice wrinkled her nose. 'That is what is confusing. Ra is the Sun god, bringing light to the world and warmth to the lifeblood of all creatures. Ra is good, but this doesn't feel all good. Good and bad it is.'

It was Ozzy's turn to shiver. 'Bad and good.'

'Well, I don't know . . .' Jack stopped short as he heard clanging in the distance. 'Oh, that must be Bone ringing for breakfast. Look, don't worry, just pop yourself in the tent, out of harm's way, and I'll come after school to check you're all right.'

'He might harm you, Jack,' said Ozzy as he climbed

through the flap in the simple canvas tent. Wraiths of green smoke billowed out as he shrank himself to fit and helped Ice in with his crook.

'Harm me he won't,' said Jack. 'I'll keep an eye out for anything funny at school – like someone new turning up, or Mr Guisely being nice to me. And please don't worry – you turn everything all green and smoky when you do.'

He peeped inside the tent. The miniature Ozzy and Ice had shuffled to the back and now looked quite like a couple of regal garden gnomes. Ozzy's crook was actually extended like a little fishing hook. Even if the tour guides looked in, they'd never guess what Ozzy and Ice actually were. But then, only another god could know what they really were. Jack just hoped that none would appear while he was at school.

After all, he would have his hands full, trying to keep up with the school basketball team.

With a sigh, Jack tied up the flaps at the front of the tent, trudged through the swirly green mists writhing across the floor of the museum and then set off for breakfast at full tilt. Nothing like a bit of Hall-Running for clearing the dog-head, he always found.

2

Jack skidded into the morning room, half expecting
to see Bone clanging two metal food servers together
like a mad monkey toy with cymbals, so loud was
the noise coming from the east wing of the house.

To his surprise, he found the room to be still and
quiet: Bone was tinkering around with a packet of
cornflakes at the end of the buffet (reserving the model
figure of a mummy for their Cluedo game, from the
looks of it); Lady Bootle-Cadogan was staring into the
middle distance over the rim of her teacup, only half
watching the tiny TV, where the weather forecaster was
chucking smiley suns around the map; his father was
poring over the *Financial Times*, occasionally dipping
the corner of it into his boiled egg.

'Who rang?' said Jack, grabbing a bagel.

'Rang? Phone? Who? Bone,' said his mother, snapping to attention. 'Bone, did you ring the bell?'

Bone pocketed the little mummy and shrugged at

the same time, indicating that no, he hadn't, and he hadn't been doing anything shifty either.

'Bell!' barked Lord Bootle-Cadogan suddenly. 'Alexander Graham Bell! Now there are some shares I should have got hold of sooner. Telephones. Telecoms. Communication,' he said, enunciating carefully as if he were talking to the insane.

'Why would you like shares in communications?'

The moment he'd asked the question Jack wanted to clamp his tongue between his teeth. Bone was shaking his head frantically from behind the cereal boxes, and the newspaper had been lowered to reveal the florid face of his father. Why couldn't he keep his mouth shut? He'd clearly walked in just after an argument – that was why his mother was silent, for goodness sake. She was only ever silent when she'd just lost a debate and was working up steam for another one.

Here it comes, he thought.

'Well, Jack, why indeed?' she spat. 'Tell him why, Jackson! Tell our dear son that it's all my fault, and that if you'd had shares in communications, you wouldn't have invested everything in those ridiculous spa pools like I suggested, and then we might be able to afford this wretched mausoleum in which we are presently – and I use the word ironically – living!' This last word was screeched down the length of the banqueting table; Lord Bootle-Cadogan raised the newspaper again as if to knock it out of the field.

Jack could hear him muttering behind the *FT*: . . . 'never listened . . .' and '. . . like Father told me . . .' and '. . . bally National Trust tea parties . . .' and some other phrases he thought he probably wasn't meant to hear.

'Gas bill?' he asked his mother. The last one had caused a near meltdown in the household – not surprisingly as it had come in at nearly £60,000.

'Worse,' whispered Lady Bootle-Cadogan. 'Minimum wages. Government rules. We have to pay all our staff minimum wages, and we have to give them all back pay right from the beginning of their contracts.'

Jack wasn't following this. 'That's good though, isn't it? Doesn't minimum mean "least"? So you have to pay all the staff the least that you can, or as little as you want, to put it simply.' It wasn't terribly nice, it was true, but it shouldn't be causing all these head-aches, surely.

'You buffoon,' blurted his father. 'We really should

13

have sent you to Eton. What ARE they teaching you at that woebegone holiday camp you call school? Don't you think I've been paying as little as I can get away with all these years? Of course I have! I don't think I've ever paid Bone a brass farthing, and you've never complained, have you, Bone?' As usual he shouted this at Bone, under the assumption that since the valet was almost mute, he must be almost deaf as well. Bone smiled weakly.

'Minimum means "at least", not "least", darling.' Jack's mother fanned herself with a napkin. 'We have to pay *at least* the industry standard to all staff, which is several pounds an hour more than we have been paying, and we have to pay them all the shortfall for the whole of their contracts.'

'As if!' bellowed Lord Bootle-Cadogan. 'We can't possibly do that. Take Bone, for example. We'd owe him a blessed fortune, seeing as his contract started in . . . when the devil was it, Bone?'

Jack winced. It had been 1919 when Albie went overseas for the first time with Lord Jay. How could he begin to explain to his parents that Bone was well over a hundred?

But his father was blathering. 'I assume you're not

14

expecting any back pay, are you, Bone? Good!' he shouted before Bone even had time to gather a suitable facial expression together. 'Because you're not getting any! Bally servants should be grateful for a roof over their head.'

'Da-ad,' said Jack slowly, 'I don't think it works like that these days . . .'

'No!' shrieked his mother. 'That's what I was saying. It doesn't work like that these days! They'll arrest you, Jackson. Not that we'd miss you at all, but . . . they might arrest me! Or Jack. We have to find the money. Where are we going to find the money?'

'Bottom of a spa pool, perhaps,' said Jack's father nastily, leaving nobody with any doubt what else he would like to find at the bottom of the spa. It could be their next Cluedo scenario: Lady Bootle-Cadogan, in the spa pool, with a rolled-up *Financial Times* . . .

'There's that noise again,' said Jack suddenly. He could hear it quite distinctly, banging and scraping away somewhere in the depths of the mansion. 'It really wasn't you, Bone.'

Told you, said Bone's face, although he was twisting his head this way and that as if seeking out the noise. He obviously couldn't hear it, and Bone's hearing was quite acute, to compensate for a century or so of appalling eyesight. Judging by the exasperated 'tut' from his father and the slightly worried tilt of his mother's head, Jack guessed that they couldn't hear it either. Even though Jack only became Anubis when he was in the crypt, sometimes his heightened senses seemed to stay with him in the real world, which could get him into trouble.

And god-dog hearing could be quite exceptional. Perhaps this was something that nobody else was meant to be able to hear. A message just for him.

Wolfing down the remains of his bagel, Jack headed for the door. 'Just got to get my school bag, Bone. Meet me out the front with the car? I don't want to be late.'

That much was true, at least – one more failure at basketball and he'd be off the team, he was sure of it, and being late was not acceptable. But if he didn't find out where that ringing was coming from, he'd go mad. Madder. Even madder than people already assumed him to be.

Jack belted through the long, shiny-floored corridors of Lowmount, down the Long Gallery, past his favourite painting of his great-grandparents, and veered off towards the east wing, where all his ancestors had preferred to have their bedrooms. Most of the staterooms were empty now, as the present family favoured a few rooms over the main kitchen that cost less to heat, but Granny Dazzle had kept her rooms over here.

For a moment Jack paused, trying to work out the source of the dinging sound that rattled around his head so loudly it was actually starting to get a bit painful. Was it in the museum? That was just back along the corridor – perhaps it was Ozzy'n'Ice trying to get his attention. If only he knew where it was he could just Zip there – his ability to zoom around at something approaching the speed of light just by picturing his destination in his head was pretty much his favourite Doghead skill. He was just about to race off when there was another clang, followed by a soft swooshing sound, from somewhere behind him.

'Granny Dazzle's room!' Spinning on his heel, he set off at a sprint towards his beloved late great-grandmother's sleeping quarters, grabbing a stuffed boar's head off the wall as he ran. If anyone was ransacking Granny D.'s rooms, they'd be sorry. Getting a boar's tusk between the eyes was not pleasant – as Jack knew from experience, having come nose to tusk with the Seth's grotesque pig-head just a few months before. OK, Boar's head or Doghead – they could choose. 'Would you rather . . .' he muttered as he shoved open the door to Granny Dazzle's suite and threw himself into the room.

The noise was deafening: *CLANG! SWOOSH! . . . SCRAPE . . . CLANG . . . SWOOSH!* Without any thoughts for his own safety, Jack followed the source of the cacophony and found himself . . . to his surprise . . . in his great-grandmother's walk-in wardrobe.

It was a mess. Clothes from every era, of every style, length, fabric and colour, were strewn all over the small room, piled in mounds and draped haphazardly across the chair, the dressing table, the door frame . . . But there was nobody here. So what was making the noise?

Suddenly Jack spotted the cause of the din, and it was only then that he realized just how ridiculously sensitized his hearing had become – in fact, just how weird his whole world had become too, even when he wasn't half-dog, half-boy.

SCRA-A-A-PE . . . a long buttoned coat he'd seen Granny Dazzle wear a couple of times for winter outings slid along the rail on its hanger, the wire hook grating along the old metal clothes rail like a fingernail on a rusty zither. Jack howled and covered his ears. *CLANG!* The clothes hanger hit the stopper at the end of the rail with a resounding *thwack* that, to Jack, reverberated as though he was standing with his head inside a church bell. Then *SWOOSH-SWOOSH* . . . the coat slid off the hanger and settled on to a coal-pile mound of discarded hats and scarves.

Jack was just trying to work out what was going on when it started again, this time with a lime-green linen suit with big yellow daisies on it that Granny Dazzle must have bought for a garden party, or perhaps for a joke. *SCRA-A-A-PE* . . . Was it possessed? Was it alive?

Wrapping one arm around his head to keep out the noise, he grabbed for the suit with his other hand. Immediately it fell off the hanger and hung limply in his hand. Hmm. Maybe it *was* possessed.

But by whom? Who on earth – or anywhere – would think this was a useful activity?

Of course. 'Granny Dazzle!' Jack shouted.

Only his mad great-granny would think that the best way to get his attention would be to chuck her old clothes at him. Naturally, she would be aware that Jack's hearing was sharp enough to catch the sound of it wherever he happened to be within the castle.

'Is that you?'

Three hatboxes flew off the shelf above his head and emptied themselves over him. Jack found himself sporting a natty pink beret that his mother had forbidden Granny Dazzle to wear in public and that she'd consequently worn whenever possible, especially if she was likely to be photographed. Jack hooted with laughter. 'Where are you? And where's Lord Jay?'

Something whispered along his cheek as more hatboxes flew off the opposite rack, and Jack found a top hat dangling from his outstretched arm. So his great-grandfather was here too. 'Why can't I see you?'

He'd witnessed both his great-grandparents in ghostly form before, and they'd been quite visible to him then. Smoky, a bit wispy perhaps, but definitely visible. Then two identical outfits swooshed along the rail like ghosts on a train, and Jack understood.

The garments were the ceremonial robes that Granny

Dazzle and the undertaker Will Waite had worn to perform the ancient rituals that sent restless souls on to the afterlife. When Granny Dazzle had died Jack and Albie had performed this ceremony on her and Lord Jay, and now it seemed that although they were probably visible in the Field of Rushes (the Ancient Egyptian version of heaven), he couldn't see them in his world.

'Oh,' he said sadly. It was great that they were there at all, of course, but a bit of a blow that he wasn't going to be able to see them, have conversations, practise his poker game . . .

So this had to be their way of spending time with him now. It was a bit weird, but to be honest his whole world was a bit weird. 'It's really sweet of you to come and see me,' he said, 'only I've got this basketball match and if I don't get there in time I'll be . . . Ow!'

Suddenly hangers were flying at him from all directions, and the noise was unbearable, even with the pink beanie rammed down over his head and stuffed into his ears. 'STOP! Please stop . . . Let me . . . Let me . . .' Let me take this stupid hat off, was what he really wanted to say, but they seemed pretty agitated.

'Let me find out what you're here for,' he finished. 'I guess you haven't just come to see me, then.'

The mound of clothes stirred as if ghostly feet had danced through them, and all at once, the large object they'd been obscuring was in clear view. It was Granny Dazzle's old portmanteau, which held all the instruments that she and, lately, Jack needed to perform their ceremonies. It shook a tiny bit as if an electrical charge had run through it, and Jack stared at it.

'You want me to move it? Where do you want it?'

It shimmied again, and the locked doors rattled on their hinges. 'You want me to open it?'

Again he felt that whispering sensation along his cheek. A kiss? It seemed he'd got it right.

There was a small problem though. 'I don't have the key at the moment. It's in the crypt – we keep it there for the ceremonies. I'll come back tonight and open it.' Then he had an idea. 'Let's do it in the crypt! I might be able to see you there. It's where Bone becomes Albie and I turn into Doghead, after all.'

This time there was a faint rustling sensation along both cheeks, and Jack grinned. 'Thanks. You go . . . um . . . home, and I'll see you later. Hopefully.'

They were gone. He could feel it. Now he could hardly wait until later to find out if he could see them again. Would he be able to get the portmanteau to the crypt without anyone noticing? Dropping to his knees, he wrapped his arms around the enormous suitcase, the size of a large chest of drawers, and heaved. It rose easily in his arms; even when he wasn't in Anubis form, some of the god-strength still coursed through his veins.

Placing the case back on the floor, Jack suddenly stared at the lock he would be opening later. He'd never noticed before, but it was a round golden door-knob set inside a larger golden circle.

Exactly like the image Ice had drawn in the air.

Jack traced it with a finger. He knew he was right. It was the sign of the Sun God. 'Ra,' he said loudly, to remind himself.

Just as the doors to the walk-in wardrobe flew wide open.

3

EGYPT, 1922

There was no mistaking it. It didn't look like what they'd been searching for, nor was it inscribed the way they might have expected, but this simple coffin was definitely it. He could feel it, right down in the marrow of his bones.

'Lord Jay,' the young man hissed in as low a voice as he could; it sounded more like a sigh than a word.

It was enough though. The older man raised his head from the tiny baby's coffin he was studying and caught Albie's eye, pausing for the merest second. Then, stretching nonchalantly, he turned his back on the rest of the antiquities team, who were foraging through the urns and shards of coffin littered around the tomb, and wandered over to Albie's side.

'Must be time for lunch,' he bellowed in his usual confident boom. Then in an undertone he added,

'You've got it?'

'Mmmm, wonder what chef has cooked up today?' said Albie, practically shouting in his nervousness. Jay glared at him, and he lowered his voice to a whisper. 'I thought I saw a hawk. It flew in here and disappeared behind this –' he jabbed with a finger – 'particular sarcophagus.'

They were in a low, cave-like tomb that held any number of coffins, some of which had crumbled away completely. This one looked as though it might go the same way soon – its silver-grey wood was flaking and rotten. Lord Jay squinted at it, then muttered from beneath his handlebar moustache, 'This one? It can't be. It's a commoner's name, and coffin.'

'That's what I thought. But then . . .'

There were scratches along the top, made by the hawk, and they seemed to point to the name chiselled by some ancient adze into the softening wood. Albie flicked his little brush casually across the letters, trying to look as if he was hardly interested in what he was doing. As they both looked on, the sarcophagus gave a barely perceptible shudder.

'Good Lord,' murmured Jay. 'Was that a mirage?'

'No,' Albie said under his breath.

Then he clamped his palms down on the coffin lid.

Even in the gloom of the burial cave, they could both sense that something was happening to the sarcophagus. The shrivelled, cracked wood shivered and grew smooth; the ashen tone strengthened through a spectrum of grey shades until it merged into a deep shining green. Shoots sprang out where the handles would have been before they rotted away, weaving themselves into a delicate trellis that bound coffin and lid together in a tight chrysalis. Just as the green hue of the coffin grew so intense that it was almost glowing, Albie tore his hands away and stuffed them into his pockets, almost expecting them to be glowing green too. The coffin reverted to its grey and broken state.

Beside him, Jay quivered, his eyes shining. For a moment he was unable to move or speak. Then 'Good,' he said hoarsely. Albie hid his pleased expression. He'd served Jay well, and that made him happy.

Pulling a monogrammed handkerchief from his pocket, Lord Jay blew his nose loudly and looked around. No one else appeared to have noticed anything unusual going on. 'What the blazes is keeping that cook today?'

'I'll go and find out,' said Albie quickly.

It was all a ruse, of course, to get everyone out of the cave while Jay had a closer look at the coffin, so Albie started rounding everyone up and moving them towards the cooking tent.

He was happy to leave Jay to it. Albie himself needed no more convincing. They'd found it; he was sure. They were the first people – ever – to find the final resting place of Osiris, Egyptian God of the Earth and the Underworld.

Joyous though the moment was, a cold hand curled itself tightly around his heart.

'Heaven help us,' muttered Albie suddenly. What chain of events had been kicked into motion? There was no telling what might happen now.

4

'Found him wearing a pink beret in my grandmother's closet, roaring at something.' Lord Bootle-Cadogan stomped up and down the front lobby. 'It's that school, I tell you!'

Jack's mother wiped a hand across her son's forehead. 'Are you hot, darling? Is it fever? What were you roaring at?'

Roaring? 'I wasn't roaring.' He didn't want to explain that he was actually saying 'Ra', as that probably wouldn't help him to persuade his parents he wasn't going mad.

'Oh, good. And the pink beret?'

He was still holding it, in fact, so there wasn't much he could do to get away with that one. Or was there . . . 'It was Granny Dazzle's favourite,' he said with a sniff. 'I just suddenly missed her.'

'He'd pulled everything on to the floor. Discipline!' barked his father. 'The boy needs discipline.'

Jack knew that this conversation, like so many others, was likely to end with the word 'Eton'. Thoughts of school reminded him that he was now officially late. He would have some serious grovelling to do in order to stay on the basketball team. 'I'm sorry, Mother, Father. I'll clear it all up when I get home. And you can ground me for . . . well, forever, if you like.' That would be OK; he never went anywhere anyway – not that they knew about.

Like a skinny guardian angel, Bone loomed up in the doorway and nodded towards the Daimler, which purred on the gravel beyond. 'Sir,' he creaked, and moved off to open the door. It took all Jack's restraint not to dive headlong into the back seat. 'Sorry,' he said again to the lobby in general. Then he deposited the pink beret on one of the hooks in the foyer and sped out to the car.

The moment they were out of sight, Jack climbed over into the passenger seat beside Bone. Bone peered at him curiously as he steered expertly towards Clearwell Comprehensive School.

'No, I wasn't trying the pink hat on,' said Jack quickly. 'It's all getting a bit weird though. Ice was talking about her sisters, and how something bad is happening to do with Ra. She did this.' He blew on the windscreen and drew the circle with a dot inside it in the mist. 'Then Granny D. and Lord Jay turn up in the wardrobe, invisible, and want us to open the portmanteau or something. And what did I find? The handle is that funny sign again – the sign of Ra.'

Bone unhinged his jaw. 'Raaaa,' he wheezed, as if trying the word for size.

'Does it mean anything to you?'

Peering hard through the windscreen, Bone scowled as if he was in pain, and Jack recognized the expression that signified Bone trying to remember something of his past.

'Never mind, Al-Bone,' he said. 'It'll all come back to you in the crypt. We're going to get the portmanteau down there tonight; I'm hoping the great-grands will be visible in there. Drop me here, will you?'

'Sir.' Bone sounded a little sarcastic. He got out of the car and shuffled around to Jack's door, then held it open for him with a low bow. 'Si-ir,' he said again.

'What's got into you?' Jack grabbed his backpack and smacked Bone in the kidneys with it so he straightened up again. 'You know you don't have to do any of that servant stuff for me any . . . oh.' So that was it. 'Did Dad offend you with all that minimum-wage stuff? I bet he did; he offended me. I don't know why he thinks he can treat people like that . . . apart from, well, he always has treated people like that and got away with it. But I'm not like that.'

Bone stared at him sulkily, then shrugged. 'Rarrr,' he said with a mischievous smirk.

'I was not roaring.' Jack smothered a smile. 'I told you, I was saying Ra.'

'Sir,' said Bone, but it came out more like 'sure.'

'I'm late,' said Jack haughtily. 'Pick me up at three thirty, will you? There's a good servant.' He didn't dare Zip to and from school – being spotted shooting by in a blur would ruin forever any chance of acceptance.

Bone blew him a loud raspberry and got back in the car. In moments Jack was on his own outside the school, so spectacularly late that even the usual late-comers were already inside or had been officially written off as absent. He traipsed into the office and picked up a late slip.

To his dismay, his least favourite teacher was poring over the registers.

'You're late, Posh Boy,' snarled Guisely, his pock-marked face almost gleeful.

'Sorry, sir.'

'Oh, don't be sorry. I'm actually relieved. Now it won't be down to me to throw you off the basketball team.'

'Sir?'

'No, your own teammates, your captain – they're going to be so fed up with you they're going to ask you to leave. I'll come with you,' added Guisely cheerfully. 'Wouldn't want to miss this.'

The worst thing, even worse than Guisely's cigarette fumes trailing him across the football pitch to the gym, was that the teacher was right. Fraser had gone to a special effort to invite him on to the team, even though Jack had once caught the ball in his teeth in an accidental doggy moment, and Jack had been delighted to be doing something almost normal, in a team, with ordinary kids. And now he'd ruined it all on his own.

The look on his team members' faces confirmed it when he pushed open the gym door and dumped his bag to one side. Fraser, especially, bore an expression of distaste and disappointment that reminded Jack horribly of his father when he'd opened the wardrobe door earlier. Behind the team captain, Minty stood aside from the other girl players and shook her head gently so her short black bob swished against her jawline.

'Jack,' said Fraser quietly, 'you were meant to be here twelve minutes ago.' He nodded to the clock above Jack's head. 'That's the third time. You know it means . . .' He didn't say it aloud, but Jack knew his next words would be – would have to be – 'You're out.'

But someone interrupted the captain. 'What's your excuse this time, Poshy?' Minty's voice was almost as gruff as Fraser's. 'Get lost again? Couldn't find your servant in time?'

Guisely sniggered at that, and Jack struggled to keep his cool. Minty, who managed to tread the line between Egyptian god and normal schoolkid far better than he ever could, was playing a part, covering up any connection between them, and stopping Fraser from chucking him off the team. He was grateful, but did she have to do 'horrible' quite so well? He decided to make her squirm, and appreciate that he had a real reason for being late. 'I overslept,' he said. 'The Sun

God,' he said slowly and deliberately, 'just didn't rise and wake me up in time. I'm sorry, Fraser.'

The other members of the team snuffled and tittered, and Minty said nastily, 'Are you for real?' But then she caught his eye and Jack gave her a little nod. Yes, he was for real.

What happened next he wasn't quite sure; one moment Jack was standing in the sports hall, watching Minty consider what he was telling her. Then she looked directly out of the window and the room went dark. There wasn't time to take it in properly – just as Jack realized that it wasn't a cloud blotting out the sunshine (as everyone else would probably think) but a pair of enormous wings belonging to a bird of prey so big that it could wrap up the entire school in its wingspan, he suddenly found himself standing outside the school in the rain.

Around him, fellow Clearwell Comp kids ran for cover, holding backpacks and jackets over their heads as they ploughed, laughing and shoving each other, towards their classrooms. Jack felt his hair. He was barely wet, but everyone else was soaked, as if they'd been caught in the deluge for much longer than he had. Puzzled, he headed into the office for his late slip, only to find Guisely walking away with the class registers – turning them to be marked. He saw Jack and smiled nastily. 'Do you need the sick bay, Posh? I assume you're ill, turning up on time like this.'

Jack stared at the clock. He was two minutes early – not just for basketball, but for school and roll-call and everything! Ignoring Guisely's stare, he sprinted to his classroom in plenty of time to avoid trouble and caught up with Minty as she followed Fraser across to basketball.

'Was that you?' he hissed. 'Turning back time and all that.'

'Well, it wasn't you,' she said. 'You're pathetic.'

'But how . . .'

'I'm a goddess, right? I have some powers to do with water and renewal. I make it rain and I can renew life for a few minutes. Simple.'

It didn't sound at all simple to Jack, but he was a god as well, when all was said and done. 'So could I have done that too?'

Minty stared at him. 'Don't make me laugh,' she said eventually with another shake of her head. 'You? Ha.'

By now they'd reached the basketball court, and to his delight Jack was able to get involved right from the beginning. Guisely eyed him suspiciously from the sidelines as if somehow aware that this wasn't quite right, and Jack fumbled his way through the first half without event.

At half-time he managed to get Minty on one side. 'I meant it about Ra, by the way. Funny stuff going on. Meet me and Albie in the crypt at sundown.'

Minty sniffed. 'I might be washing my hair.'

'Don't you mean your hawk?' Her hawk was part of her, really, as Amentet, Goddess of the Dead, when it wasn't blocking out the sun and causing downpours. Jack grinned at his own joke, but . . .

'Like I said, you're not funny.' With a withering glance Minty handed him the ball and walked away, but behind her back she held up eight fingers.

Eight o'clock. Sundown. She'd be there.

Might as well make it a full house, Jack decided later. Albie, Jack and Minty; Granny Dazzle and Lord Jay – all the old gang, together again. They just needed Ozzy'n'Ice to complete the set.

'Al-Bone,' he said as they drove home from school,

'let's call by the museum and tell Ozzy'n'Ice what's been going on.'

'Sir.' Bone changed direction on to the back road that circled the graveyard. They entered the museum from the crypt, which would raise fewer questions.

It was a good job nobody was around to witness them arriving. As he opened the door to the museum, Jack found himself fighting off a terrified four-armed creature, and it wasn't until he realized that two arms were green and two were palest white that he worked out what the creature actually was.

'Ice'n'Ozzy, Ozzy'n'Ice, calm down!'

With Bone's help, he separated them and sat each of them down on a camp stool. 'What is going on?'

'He has been,' squeaked Ice.

'Been he has.' Ozzy pointed upward, and all four raised their eyes to the ceiling. In blood – Jack didn't want to think about whose – was the now familiar sign of Ra: a circle with a dot inside it.

And through it was scored an enormous bloody X.

'Oh, flipping hairy pigs, he's back again,' said Jack with a groan.

5

It wasn't just the ceiling that was damaged. The whole museum was a bit of a mess, now Jack came to look at it. Several of the glass cabinets had been blown out, the artefacts within them sucked through the shattered remains and hanging out like intestines. The camping scene was pretty devastated too, with the tent completely ripped in two. He could picture it being torn asunder and cast aside to reveal two shivering garden gnomes . . .

Jack clambered on to the camp bed and wondered whether to ask Ozzy and Ice to make it fly as they sometimes did. But with his hand outstretched, he could just about touch the ceiling. His finger smeared the bloody outline of the Ra sign and he quickly withdrew it.

'Have to clean that off in a while. Who was it, and what did they want?' he said, noticing that Ozzy had faded to a pale lime shade. 'They obviously frightened the life out of you. Or the colour, at least.'

'It was Seth, in spirit. The pig-head appeared on the ceiling and spun, and then scored that pattern you see into the plaster.'

'Appeared on the ceiling, it did,' Ice echoed shakily.

'So that's his own blood,' said Jack. 'Good.' Well, maybe not so good, as he now had Seth blood on his hand. Oddly, when he held out his finger, it was just wet, not bloody and red. He wiped it on his trousers anyway, and the moisture evaporated instantly.

' Royal blood it might be,' said Ice. 'This is what he said . . .' And she passed him an ancient papyrus, crumbling at the edges yet smeared with fresh moist blood. As Jack watched, the blood ebbed back towards the edge, leaving a clear tidemark behind it.

With Bone hovering close by, Jack unrolled it carefully, not because he was worried it might disintegrate, but because there was every chance an evil pig would leap out of the page and grab him in its tusky jaws. 'Ah, it's a rhyme.'

Seth appeared to like rhymes: he'd cursed the Bootle-Cadogans and Cornthwaites in verse in 1922, and here was another. Jack read it aloud.

'Ra's Day of Sun will bring back Seth,
Through uncrowned Osiris of the Earth.
And none can turn the tide of death,
Except a son of royal birth.'

'We are doomed,' whispered Ice.

'Doomed we are,' agreed Ozzy glumly.

'Well, you are with that kind of attitude,' said Jack. 'Wow! I sounded just like my father then. Sorry.'

'But I have no crown,' said Ozzy, tipping his head so they could look into the gaping hole in his skull. 'He will attack. I will die again. We must hide.'

'Hide we must,' confirmed Ice.

Jack sighed. He could understand their reaction – Seth was always turning up and trying to destroy Ozzy, and it must be tempting just to get out of his way. 'But if you give in without trying, then Seth gets to win and –' he consulted the papyrus again – 'he'll be back with a tide of death. That can't be good, can it? What would a tide of death look like? A tsunami?'

Bone rubbed his chin morosely, then pointed to something on the floor. It was the husk of a dead insect. 'What is that – a grasshopper?' said Jack.

Ice sucked in a breath. 'It is a locust.'

'A locust it is,' said Ozzy.

Jack peered at it. 'It's a bit ugly, but if that's all the tide of death is, I don't think we need to be worried. I mean, we dealt with bugs before – remember Wormwood Moonshiner?'

But Bone had turned even paler than usual, and Ozzy covered the hole in his head without even thinking. 'It is not just one like the Moonshiner beetle,' he said softly. 'It is many.'

'Many millions it is,' added Ice.

'Many millions of millions.'

'Ah,' said Jack. 'You mean like a plague.'

'Many plagues,' said Ozzy sadly. 'Plagues attacking the earth because I am uncrowned.'

'A tide of death.' Jack nodded. He had a vague memory of some plagues that had affected Egypt. Locusts, and what else was it? He'd have to look it up.

He prodded Ozzy in the shoulder. 'Don't give up. We just need to work it all out, and find your crown, and a . . . um . . . son of royal birth.' OK, that last bit might prove a tad difficult, but Jack was at least willing to give it a go. Everyone else seemed to have fallen at the first hurdle. 'We'll meet at the crypt at eight to discuss it all properly. Bone, go and grab the portmanteau and hoick it over there; I'll head the parents off. Ozzy'n'Ice, take the crumbly paper and, er, get a grip, OK?'

As everyone rallied to their duties, Jack scampered along the corridor to his mother's study. It was where he usually found her at the end of the school day, staring anxiously at her computer screen while Roger, their old gun dog, dribbled on her feet. Today was no different, except that when Jack entered the room, Roger growled.

'Roger, it's me, what are you growling at?' Jack went to pat the great wizened head but withdrew his hand quickly when Roger snarled viciously.

'Mum, what's wrong with Roger?'

'He does seem to have taken rather a dislike to you all of a sudden.' Lady Bootle-Cadogan sighed. 'Everybody's cross these days. Even Roger. And the weatherman.' The screen in front of her showed the weather report for the next few days, and the weatherman, who had been flinging sunny faces around before, was now looking rather flustered as the spikes around the outside of the suns kept dropping off on to the floor, leaving just a yellow circle with a dot in the middle. Jack went to point to the screen, then quickly stopped himself. Now was not the time to explain to his mother about the sign of Ra, and, more worryingly, he had caught a glimpse of himself reflected in the computer screen.

He felt his chin quickly. Stubble! His dog-head was reappearing. No wonder Roger was alarmed – he probably sensed his alpha-dog status being threatened by Jack.

Jack backed out of the room hastily, saying, 'Don't worry about dinner – I'm going to do my homework in the museum so I'll take something down there with me.'

'All right, darling. Eat some fruit,' said his mother wearily. 'At least we have an orchard so that doesn't cost us anything.'

To appease her, Jack grabbed an apple from the kitchen and fought the temptation to throw it and scamper after it. His super-sharp teeth were through it in no time, and he snapped through the core and ate that too in a matter of seconds. His legs felt jittery, like a wound-up coil – full Doghead status was going to be upon him fairly soon, he could tell. Perhaps it was the reappearance of Seth that had triggered it – for some time now he'd only been jackal-headed in the crypt, but now it looked as though he might be hairy and black more of the time.

Pent-up energy surged through his thighs, and as if they were sensing his dogginess emerging, the skulk of jackals that lived over at the graveyard started to howl. Now he felt worse than ever – if he didn't run this off he'd be unbearable in the meeting later on. Jack checked his watch. Ten to six. He had a couple of hours spare. A sprinting dog-god could get a long way in two hours . . .

Glad that it was already dusk, Jack bounded twice around the perimeter of Lowmount Hall, making sure to sniff out any new smells that might show where Seth was hiding out. After the second turn around the grounds and a quick snuffle in the antique shop housed in an old barn at the edges – rats and the odd chicken, but no pigs, he decided – Jack checked his watch again. Five past six.

'Not fair,' groaned Jack. He must have run about twenty miles, but it had taken less than a quarter of an hour. Furthermore, his legs felt no less tense than before. He could have played his hamstrings like a violin, they were so taut. So off he went again, in bigger and bigger circles – around the grounds, around the village, around the trees surrounding the village, springing along like a greyhound in a low, sinuous run that made him look more jackal than boy.

Seven o'clock. He still had an hour to kill, and a fully-charged battery in each of his thigh muscles. 'This is getting ridiculous!' There was nothing else for it. He'd have to head out of town. The straightest route was directly along the motorway. Making his way to the sloping bank beside the motorway, Jack turned his back resolutely on the signs that might take him towards Windsor, and therefore Eton. He'd head towards South Wales. That was a long way away.

Off he went, vaulting fences and ditches, hidden from view by the motorway verge and the night closing in. It felt good to be out in the open, streaming through the balmy evening with such speed that the wind felt cool and welcome as it ruffled his hair. Fur. Just for fun, he Zipped across the Severn Bridge in a blue-black streak that might have been mistaken for a storm cloud and shot through the toll barrier at the Welsh end. His powers must be getting stronger – he wasn't just covering counties now, but countries. Barely pausing for breath, Jack turned back towards the English end of the bridge and Zipped his way down the central reservation.

He felt less excitable now, and was able to slow his running to a more normal speed – normal for him, which was still like an express train. Bored with the motorway, he plunged off into the undergrowth and ran back towards home through the outskirts of several other villages, following the scent that told him he was heading for Lowmount – a combination of mellow brick, jasmine and mothballs from Granny Dazzle's clothes. He wasn't far now; another fifteen miles and he'd be skirting Lowmount village.

He was in a forest – in fact, he was more deeply hidden within a forest than he had realized. Far to the east he could hear the sound of televisions – probably Greenhithe village, if his directions were correct. Off to the west it was his sense of smell that was more engaged. Sausages. Hundreds of them. The scent was unbearably good; Jack was pretty sure drool was hanging from his mouth in long strings as he turned his head to sniff it up.

Tracking the scent, Jack took off through the trees, the aroma of grilled sausage nearly driving him mad.

Why did they never have sausages at home? Why couldn't they just have beans on toast, or spag bol, or the stuff that the other kids at school ate, instead of big fussy meals with different courses and piles of accompaniments? Eating like a lord was not as much fun as people might imagine . . .

The smell was upon him, forcing saliva to practically squirt out of his mouth. To be getting such an extreme reaction, his dog-head must be more pronounced than ever. Whoever was cooking such a mountain of sausages would get the fright of their life if they saw him. Slowing to a halt, Jack crept behind a tree and peered through to see where the source of the mesmerizing smell lay.

It wasn't a village. Not a normal one, anyway. It took Jack a while to work out what it was, exactly, when all he could see were identical wooden chalets, with identical outdoor eating areas, and identical families of mum, dad, two kids and a baby all cooking up a storm on the identical barbecues that were tucked under the eaves of the chalets. Nearly every chalet had a father flipping sausages and burgers while the mother passed around bread rolls and ketchup. Jack had never seen anything more delicious in his life. Had he *ever* seen his father grill a sausage? His mum tossing bread rolls about and having food fights with the tomato sauce? Never!

But that was because they'd never been to a holiday park. All their holidays prior to the last few years had been in exotic hot spots or glamorous ski resorts. Recently Lord Bootle-Cadogan had insisted that when one lived in paradise, there was no need to go elsewhere on holiday. It had taken a while before Jack realized that this was just an excuse; they couldn't actually afford to go on their expensive holidays any more.

'I'd settle for this, Dad,' said Jack, watching enviously as a boy of about five or six at the nearest chalet squeezed tomato sauce and French mustard down his chin as he wrestled with a charred hot dog. It looked perfect.

Jack felt as though he could stand there forever, even if it made him insane with hunger, but suddenly an announcement from some nearby loudspeaker made him jump high in the air. 'Holidaymakers, please note that the wave pool will close at eight o'clock. Ten minutes to closing, everyone.' The man making the announcement sounded bored beyond belief and a little out of breath – not like someone who ever used the wave pool, or any other pool. 'I repeat, the wave pool closes at eight o'clock.'

'No, it can't be!' hissed Jack. Nearly eight o'clock? If he was late for Minty one more time this week he might just find himself dead. He sucked in one last, longing lungful of sausagey air, then suddenly his breath sharpened. There! Off to his left was an unmistakable stench.

'Pig,' he growled. He had smelt it once before when the disgusting mouth of Seth's pig-head had nearly swallowed up the crypt, after first disgorging all manner of hideous creatures from its slimy depths. Seth was nearby, he just knew it.

With no time to linger, he spun around and Zipped back to the crypt, passing through trees and stone walls and the odd parked car as if they were no more solid than the warm evening air.

Jack arrived with one minute to spare, and very glad he was too since Minty was already there. In fact, he was the last to arrive. Ozzy and Ice were perched like bookends on Granny Dazzle's sarcophagus, with Albie leaning dispiritedly across it in the space between them. Minty and her hawk were amusing themselves by snuffing out candles and then relighting them with a touch of Minty's stubby fingernail – another trick Jack hadn't known she could do – while Granny Dazzle and Lord Jay floated overhead, both looking incredibly wispy. The portmanteau was open on the altar steps, and although its presence didn't seem to have done anything to make his great-grandparents more solid, Jack could at least see them.

Jack cleared his throat. 'Hello, did anybody bring anything to eat? I'm starving.'

Albie glared at him for a second then slid a sandwich across the plaque on Granny Dazzle's tomb. 'I had made it for myself, seeing as I was cleaning the Daimler until late, but if you're hungry, Oh lord and master, I suppose you should have it.'

'I'll make you one later,' promised Jack, stuffing it into his face whole. He'd never felt so famished. 'I just smelt all these sausages being cooked at the holiday park, and it's made me completely ravenous.'

Minty raised one eyebrow. 'Holiday park? I can see you're taking this very seriously.'

'Actually, I was tracking Seth,' said Jack quickly, although that had only been a small part of what he'd been up to.

The mention of his name sent Ozzy and Ice into their wailing and thrashing routine. Albie had to spring out of the way so that he wasn't pinioned between them like the meat in his sandwich. Jack shook his head; sometimes it was hard to imagine that they were gods who'd had almost complete control of the underworld.

'Calm down,' he said with a grin. 'His scent wasn't very strong, so he's not too close or too big, wherever he is. But,' he added, 'he's clearly around, and he's going to cause trouble. Granny Dazzle, is that why you're here?'

The faint outlines of his great-grandparents nodded furiously, wafting across to the portmanteau and rattling the hinges.

'They keep doing that,' said Albie. 'It's getting rather wearing. Like Marley's ghost in *A Christmas Carol*.'

Jack's poor old relatives were clearly doing their best to open the portmanteau further and get something out of it. They just didn't have the . . . well, the body, Jack supposed, to do it properly. Now he thought about it, there seemed to be a lack of oomph in the room as a whole: Albie was lolling around scowling into the middle distance, Minty was clearly bored out of her skull, and Ozzy'n'Ice appeared to have lost the will to live.

'What's wrong with everyone?' said Jack abruptly. 'Come on, we've beaten him before, and we'll beat him again. A plan, that's what we need.'

'So you're giving us orders now?' said Albie.

'No.' He wasn't, was he? It didn't feel like he was being bossy, but just in case he altered his tone. 'Let's have a think about that poem again, and just . . . um . . . volunteer some suggestions on what to do.'

He read the poem aloud again, and then they all stared at each other glumly, even Granny D. and Lord Jay, who appeared to have sat down on the portmanteau.

'Right,' said Jack, trying to be extra cheerful. 'Uncrowned Osiris of the Earth – that's pretty clear. You've got a hole in your head, Ozzy. Do you think you and Ice could try finding your missing piece again?'

Ozzy shrugged. 'We can look, I suppose.'

'Look I suppose we can,' agreed Ice, although she seemed no more confident than Ozzy.

'Good, that's a start, well done,' said Jack, with more enthusiasm than usual. It seemed necessary at the moment. 'Albie, do you want to help your old buddy Jay?'

Albie stared at him, then at the ghost of Jay, then back at Jack. 'Naturally,' he said slowly, and Jack was surprised to hear a tone of deep sarcasm.

'OK,' he said slowly, 'maybe you can go through the portmanteau with them, as they can't seem to get hold of what they need, and check things off one by one.'

'Maybe I can,' said Albie. 'All right, I will.'

What was up with him? Jack watched as Albie sauntered over to the portmanteau, reached straight through Jay's knees and pulled out a leathery calf's leg. He looked as though he'd like to club Jay to death with it if he wasn't already dead. The ghosts of his grandparents both shook their heads, and Albie thrust the leg back through Jay's ghostly thigh and went on to the next item. Blimey, he was in a mood, thought Jack.

'That leaves you and me, Minty,' he said, far more cheerfully than he felt. Minty was a bit of an unknown quantity, really – sometimes friendly, often nasty, and constantly keeping him guessing as to what side she was really on.

'Hurray,' she said flatly.

Hmm, she was a bit on the nasty side at the moment. He'd better go easy on her. 'So what would we like to do?'

'Hathor, go and get it,' said Minty. The hawk swooped off Minty's head and grabbed the papyrus from his hands, then hovered in front of Minty so she could read it. 'What's left? Stopping the tide of death – well, I actually like dead people. It's my job to welcome them once they've passed over. A tide of death might be fun.'

'Oh,' said Jack. She was off again, confusing him – did that mean she liked killing people too?

'I'm joking,' she said suddenly. 'I'd rather not be too busy, thank you. Why don't we find out more about the son of royal birth?'

'Yes!' said Jack, relieved. 'And the plagues. We could use the Internet. But Mum was on the computer last time I looked, and she could be there for hours. How about we use the school library in the morning instead?'

Minty waited as Hathor settled herself on to the little round skullcap on her head and dipped a claw over the edge into her dark hair. 'Yes, Hathor's just shown me an image of your mother through the study window. She looks like she's in for the night. OK, we'd better use the library. Half past eight. Don't be late. And don't even think about pointing out that I just rhymed.'

Jack had been just about to comment on it, and on the whole business of how Hathor transferred images to her brain, so he bit his tongue. 'Ow.'

Really, everybody was very crotchety at the moment. It was beginning to wear off on him too. Rather disgruntled, Jack excused himself and headed off to bed. Via the kitchen to find some food – Roger's Pedigree Chum, if he was lucky.

6

To any casual observer, they looked just like common-or-garden archaeologists, grubbing around in the desert, trying to find any tomb that hadn't already been looted by the locals – or, worse, discovered by another archaeologist. They didn't appear excited, just hot and dusty and a trifle fed up.

Lord Bootle-Cadogan knocked grains of sand out of his extravagant moustache, almost directly into the face of Albie, who was kneeling below him, digging in a lacklustre fashion at the edges of the excavation. 'Do you know what I'm thinking, Cornthwaite?' boomed Lord Jay. 'We've gone through the whole site now and found nothing of interest. We might as well move on. Let's pack up over the next day or two and head back to Luxor.'

Albie sighed deeply and nodded, tucking his little trowel into the back pocket of his pale linen suit. He stood and stretched, waiting as his lord and master called off the teams of locals who had trailed after them from Luxor central, hoping for money, work, artefacts to sell . . .

'There's nothing here,' he said carefully to the nearest of the locals, a young boy who had attached himself to the team, serving as translator and general dogsbody and trying to make himself indispensable. 'We go now.'

'That is sad.' The boy gazed at him imploringly. 'I stay. I translate for you.'

'Nothing to translate,' said Lord Jay, overhearing. He clapped a large hand on the boy's shoulder. 'Good work, Adjo. But we've found nothing, the antiquities licence to dig has nearly come to an end and the money's run out now. We have to go home. And so do you.'

'Home is with you, sir,' insisted the boy, but Jay had already moved away, removing the little wooden marker posts from the edges of the site and pointing down the hill to the waiting camel train.

Albert Cornthwaite grabbed the boy's hand and shook it firmly. 'Well done, Adjo, really. We couldn't have got this far without you.' It was more true than he could say: without Adjo explaining what his name meant, Albie might never have recognized the contents of the unassuming coffin.

'But where have you got? Nowhere.' The boy's disappointment was evident. 'I have been letting you down.'

'It's just the way it goes in this game, my friend,' said Albie. He could hardly stand to see the boy's misery. Barely three years younger than Albie, Adjo was already the head of his family, and this loss of income would be quite devastating to them. Albert knew exactly how that felt, but they had to pretend the dig was over. 'We dig, and sometimes we find something. This time it was not to be. Lord Jay will make sure you are properly compensated, I promise you. But there's no point in staying if there's absolutely nothing here.'

'I know it. I am strong. I will find new work.' Adjo sounded more confident than he looked, and Albie cursed inwardly at the need for deception. The first thing they had to do was to get everybody else away before they realized what was here, beneath their feet . . .

He watched the boy's back as he trudged away down the dune. Even the set of his thin shoulders beneath his long white overshirt showed how miserable he was.

'I didn't sign up for this, Jay,' he said to his travelling companion. 'I had no idea that archaeology would mean so much subterfuge. Lying to people that I like, who deserve better. It's really not on.'

'Wishing you hadn't come, Albie?' Lord Jay shot him a mischievous grin. 'I could have brought your brother instead, you know. He's incredibly bright too. Maybe I will next time.'

Albie snorted. 'Over my dead body.'

'Oh, I don't think it will come to that,' said Lord Jay.

Albie squinted at him suspiciously. It sounded as though Jay was seriously considering it . . .

7

The alarm went off at seven, and Jack woke lying on his front with his chin on his hands. 'Oh no.' That wasn't a good sign.

Springing out of bed, he raced to the mirror, and a fine canine head glared back at him. From his neck upward, every spare bit of flesh was covered in blue-black velvety fur. His nose had extended so far that from where he was standing it actually touched the mirror, glistening like a piece of wet jet. His ears too were black and pointy. He was, in fact, Doghead.

He'd skip breakfast with his parents. He had to get to school in time to use the library before registration. Bone would have to help.

But what if his parents spotted him anyway? First of all, he had to be dressed so that they couldn't see his head if they bumped into him, so he grabbed a scarf from his winter closet, wrapped it around his muzzle and jammed a baseball cap down on top of his ears.

It was sweltering; outside the sun was already beating steadily and the thermometer rising above twenty degrees. If his mother saw him, she'd have a fit.

'Shut up,' he said to his stomach, which was rumbling madly. 'You'll have to wait. I can't go to breakfast like this.'

His mother would want to know why though. Jack thought about it for a moment, then caught a familiar whiff and inspiration struck. Hauling on the rest of his uniform, he checked the corridor and followed the scent of Doris. As the scent sharpened he stopped behind a stuffed stag's head, then peeked out to where the guide was carefully straightening the cards on a display of war medals. She'd put her walkie-talkie down on a nearby seat. In less than a second, Jack had pictured it, Zipped across to the chair, picked up the walkie-talkie and then Zipped back around the corner, out of sight and sound.

'Mother,' he said as clearly as he could with canine jaws, 'are you there?'

There was a crackle and then Lady Bootle-Cadogan's surprised voice rattled out from the intercom. 'Jack? Is this what we are reduced to? Communicating by walkie-talkie?'

'Sorry, Mum, but I've just remembered I've got to be at school early. I'll Zip . . . head straight over to Bone's and grab something to eat in the car.'

His mother's sigh sounded like static interference. 'Oh well. That does make sense. I'm terribly busy anyway – have to be at the spa-pool place by nine. Make sure Bone's back with the car before then, will you?'

'Will do. Over and out.' Jack Zipped back around the stag's head, wedged the walkie-talkie in its horns and then headed out across the meadows to Bone's gate.

It was a good job that he hadn't pictured Bone's front door in his mind's eye. To his surprise, he wasn't the first one there. Lord Bootle-Cadogan was standing in Bone's doorway, wagging a finger at Bone who looked more ancient and bowed than ever, squinting even in the early sunshine, which was weakened by the arrival of a flurry of grey clouds. At the rattle of the wooden gate, both men jumped and then stared up the path.

'Good Lord,' spat Jack's father. 'It's the hottest day of the year and you're wearing a scarf! Is your acne really that bad, boy?'

'Morning, Dad,' called Jack cheerfully. 'No, no, it's not acne, it's . . . um . . . just a project we're doing at school. The Industrial Revolution, and how it transformed, er, knitting. There's no room in my bag for the scarf so I just thought I'd wear it.'

His father looked him up and down with disgust. 'I'm not sure I approve of your fascination with knitwear, Jack. Not natural. I'm sure it's the influence of all those bally girls at your school.'

Hang on, thought Jack. The hat yesterday. The scarf today. He could see where his father was coming from. Even more worryingly, he could see where he would be going too – straight to an insistence that if he wanted a good collection of woollen goods, including socks, hats and scarves, he could bally-well go to Eton, where they had those things in bally truckloads . . .

'Anyway, what are you doing here?' he said hastily. Better to distract his father than argue himself into a corner.

'Never you mind.' Lord Bootle-Cadogan nodded curtly to Bone. 'That's between me and Bone. You think on it, Bone. There may be no alternative.' With that, he cast one last disparaging glance at Jack's neck and strode off to his idling Land Rover. Bone stared after him with such potent evil in his violet eyes that Jack wondered if Seth had possessed him.

'Blimey, what did he say to you?'

Bone glared at Jack, who quailed a little. Then the manservant broke into a series of mimes, leaping up and down and tugging at an imaginary forelock, serving pretend food, brushing down clothes, driving a fake car, all with that same malevolent sheen to his eyes and a great sneer plastered over his lips. At the end, he turned to Jack, opened both palms upward, then looked at the great pile of nothingness he was holding with what appeared to be tears in his eyes.

'Oh. You've done all this work for all these years and never been paid for it?'

Bone gave a tiny nod. Then he put a hand on his chest.

'I know. You did it for love – for Granny Dazzle.' Jack felt terrible. What could he say that would make it any better? Certainly not what he had to say next. 'Thing is though, Bone, I need a shave, and I was wondering if you could do it for me before I go to school . . . I'll understand if you don't want to.'

After a brief pause, during which Bone studied Jack with an expression he couldn't quite fathom, the valet

stood back and jerked his head along the corridor.
'Come in.'

It was quite an alarming shave, with Bone brandish-
ing the cut-throat razor in a spiky, angry fashion, but
fifteen minutes later Jack towelled his face clean and
touched his chin. Smooth again. It probably wouldn't
last long, and he'd have to keep the scarf on to cover
his nose, but it would give him enough time to get to
school and use the computer. Then later, he could
find out just what his father had been offering – or
withdrawing – to make his friend so upset.

'Thanks, Al-Bone. Meet me in the crypt after school
and tell me what my dear old pops was saying . . .'

But Bone shook his head. This one was personal,
it seemed. Between him and the current Lord Bootle-
Cadogan. He put his hands either side of an imaginary
steering wheel and wiggled them back and forth.

'OK, I do need a lift. Thanks. We're . . . We're not
the same, you know, me and my father,' he added
suddenly. Of course, Bone – his friend Albie – knew
that. Didn't he? He didn't look particularly keen to
talk anything through with his buddy Jack – but maybe
that was just a boy thing.

Sure enough, Bone didn't utter a sound all the way

to school, and while that wasn't so unusual for a person who was nearly mute, he usually had a few mimes to share with Jack. Jack headed up the school drive feeling a little disconcerted, like a small black cloud was following him. When Fraser caught up with him, Jack brushed him off quite quickly.

'Hi, Frase. Sorry, I'm late for . . . something. No surprise there then.'

Fraser squinted at him suspiciously. 'You're not joining the cricket team, are you?'

'Not unless you're kicking me off the basketball team,' said Jack with a laugh.

Fraser's expression silenced him.

'Wow. You're kicking me off the basketball team, aren't you?'

'Erm, sorry, it's just that . . . some of the guys think you're a bit unreliable,' muttered Fraser uncomfortably.

Jack spun round at the library door. 'Which guys?'

'Just . . . some of them.'

'Guys? Or Minty?' said Jack crossly.

'She's one of them,' said Fraser, scuffing the ground with the toe of his trainer. 'Just try to be on time next time, and in your gear. What's with the scarf?'

'Well, it might just be me, but it's suddenly a bit CHILLY,' said Jack crossly.

What was up with everyone this morning? Grey skies, grey moods, and all his friends getting on at him for stuff that wasn't even his fault. Turning away abruptly, he rattled through the revolving library door and sought out Minty's shiny black swag of hair.

'Oi, Hawk-head,' he hissed. 'Why are you stirring things up with Fraser? You know I love basketball. It's the only normal thing I do!'

Minty moved her bag so he could sit down next to her at the computer. 'Calm down,' she growled softly. 'I'm only thinking of you – you'll probably be a bit busy in the next few weeks, that's all.'

'Well, I can be busy AND normal,' said Jack. Honestly, didn't any of them have lives? Afterlives? The school bell rang. 'Go on, do your little rain dance. We need about ten minutes,' he said abruptly.

Minty stared at him for a long, icy moment, then she averted her gaze to the windows and blinked a couple of times. The shadows outside deepened into a hawk-shape and raindrops spattered on the windows.

Jack's bad mood lifted immediately. 'You might not

be normal, but that was pretty cool.'

'Thanks,' said Minty shortly. 'Now, did it hurt to be nice?'

'No.' Jack thought about it for a moment. 'I think I was a bit rude to Fraser.'

'Fraser,' said Minty, pointing down the driveway, 'hasn't even arrived yet, or had any kind of conversation with you.'

It was true. Fraser and Bailey were sheltering under a large sycamore tree at the gate, waiting for the rain to abate. Jack stared at the burgeoning tree. He didn't even remember seeing it before; Minty's rain must have made it flourish like that. 'Yep. Really cool,' he said to Minty. 'Sorry.'

'Stop apologizing, you big drip, or I'm going to have to punch you.' Minty turned back to the computer. 'Work to do.'

Jack fished the papyrus out of his bag and spread it on his knee so he could read the verse.

'Ra's Day of Sun will bring back Seth,
Through uncrowned Osiris of the Earth.
And none can turn the tide of death,
Except a son of royal birth.'

'Where do we start?' he said. 'Ra's Day of Sun? What's that, Sunday? If so, which Sunday?'

'I know this already,' said Minty, pushing a lock of black hair behind her ear. She looked so much like an ordinary and scary schoolgirl that it was hard to remember she was an Egyptian goddess. 'This is why our pharaohs had their tombs built in the way they did, in a pyramid shape with mirrors and shafts to let in the light of Ra on the Day of Sun. On that day, the Nile would refill, the trees turn green and the lands become fruitful once more. Osiris, the God of Agriculture, among other things, would take over his duties and bring forth a bountiful harvest for the pharaoh and his people.'

'So . . . it's quite a special day then?'

'A day of great celebrations.'

Jack grinned. 'How do gods celebrate?'

This time it was Minty's turn to grin. 'We play basketball. Properly.'

'Is that another dig at me?'

Minty stared at him, exasperated. 'Stop being so sensitive, you great big girl.'

'I'm not . . .' started Jack. But he was. Definitely oversensitive. He took a deep breath. 'OK, what's special about this day? I mean, how come it gets chosen as the Day of Ra Ra Ra celebrations and all that?'

'It is the summer solstice.'

'Makes sense.' Jack brought up the search engine on the Internet and keyed in 'summer solstice'. 'June twenty-first,' he announced. 'The longest day of the year in the northern hemisphere. Sun worshippers everywhere really love it. Get the barbecue out. Top up the tan. Quite often they come to Lowmount for a day trip.'

'It is so much more than that.'

Jack pointed to the date on the computer. 'And it's less than a week away.'

So that was that bit translated – the Day of Sun was 21 June – in just a few days' time. Uncrowned Osiris of the Earth also stacked up: Ozzy was still missing the crown of his head. Now for the son of royal birth – a king or prince, he supposed.

'How are we going to get a member of the royal family involved? he said. 'We don't even have a king, we have a queen.'

'You'd better work fast on an alternative then,' said Minty, pointing towards the clock. There was only five minutes left to registration, and outside the students were scurrying through the sudden rainfall to their classrooms. 'Maybe the king of another country?'

Jack considered it for a moment, then typed carefully into the search engine: English throne succession. 'I don't really know how many countries have royal families. But . . . well, the next monarch here will be a king.'

'Oh, well done, genius. You could have saved us ten minutes.'

'Well, you can just recreate ten minutes, can't you?'

'Yes, but I have to keep making it rain.'

'This is England – we're used to rain.'

'Yes,' roared Minty, suddenly terrifying, 'but the Egyptians aren't! And it's not much good for the appearance of Ra!'

Jack sat back in his chair. Enough was enough. 'Honestly, what is up with everyone at the moment? Every person I know – and quite a few gods and ghosts – keeps having tantrums. I hate it!'

He was just about to pick up his bag and stomp off when Minty grabbed his arm. 'You're right. This is his doing.'

'Seth?'

'His presence is already blocking Ra. Without the

sun there is only gloom. It's putting everyone in a bad mood.'

'Well, it might not be a tide of death, but I still don't like it.' Jack stared grumpily at the computer screen, about to key in 'plagues', and then suddenly sat forward. 'Oh my life.'

This was unbelievable. Unreal but true. 'It says here that the person who's second-in-line to the throne is Prince William.'

'Makes sense,' said Minty. 'But what's so interesting about him?'

'Well, apart from the fact he's going to be king one day,' said Jack, rolling his eyes, 'he's got a rather special birthday.'

They both stared at the date on the screen. Prince William's birthday was just a few days away. On 21 June: the summer solstice.

The Day of Ra.

'The son of royal birth,' said Jack. 'Prince William. And we're going to have to . . . to kidnap him.'

'No problem,' said Minty casually.

He wouldn't put it past her. 'To use your phrase: don't even think about it,' he said. 'This one has to come from me.'

8

His tall frame, slight build and pale skin were very well suited to the damp English countryside, and though his training as an undertaker had required him to do some heavy lifting at times (of bodies that were literally dead weights), nothing he'd done so far could begin to compare with the task facing him now: hauling an enormous sarcophagus. Along a subterranean tunnel. In suffocating heat. This was not going to be easy.

He stood back and considered the task at hand. It was lucky that the sarcophagus was plain, not encased in gold or lead or anything else that might weigh it down still further. The roughly hewn wooden crate was unadorned, and even though it had been prised open and looted, it was likely that the thieves had been disappointed, as there was very little in the way of ornamentation contained within or without – just the bones of a skeleton with a large hole in the top of its skull. That made sense to Jay and Albie: legend had it that Osiris had been murdered and chopped up by his brother Seth, and the body parts flung to the far corners of the earth. The odd missing chunk was hardly a surprise in those circumstances. And the unadorned coffin was a good decoy, putting off many other archaeologists – and Seth – in their search for Osiris's resting place.

When Albie started to push the coffin he was surprised to find that it slid with relative ease along the sandy floor of the tunnel, since the withered bones within weighed practically nothing. The wooden crate itself seemed almost to float, it was so light and cleverly made. As the light from the narrow shafts cut into the roof faded, Albie wedged a torch beneath the lid of the coffin, so it shone ahead of him down the tunnel like the gas headlights on the old hansom cabs in London. They glided along without incident, just as though Albie was pushing a vegetable cart through an East End market.

And then suddenly the flame guttered. A breeze. He quickly shielded the torch before it blew out completely and plunged him and his strange companion into complete darkness, then held it out in front of him. Now it illuminated what lay ahead – a fork in the tunnel.

Albie investigated the openings in turn. One led down and to the right, and it would have been relatively easy to let the sarcophagus slide along ahead of him down this passage. The other, to the left, was narrower and seemed to take an upward trend. It would be a squeeze. Difficult. Unbearable in this ungodly heat.

So of course that was the way he'd have to go.

And of course Jay wasn't here to help.

He'd discovered more and more lately that this was the way things went. Jay was what he liked to call 'the face' of the operation, meaning that he supplied the money and expertise and smiled for the journalists (and a few dancing girls, one in particular). Albie, ironically, was the 'muscle', according to Jay. In other words, he did all the work.

Jay did have a point in this particular instance: if Lord Jay Bootle-Cadogan had been seen ferreting around near a dig that they'd abandoned because it was supposedly empty, suspicions would have been aroused. The other archaeologists, especially, were very intrigued to know what Lord B-C was up to, and so were a couple of the more astute journalists. Albie, on the other hand, aroused no interest whatsoever. This was nothing new – no one had ever taken an interest in him, apart from Lord Jay, who had recognized his clever analytical brain and decided to act as his sponsor and mentor.

Anyway, there was no point getting sniffy about it now. He'd promised Jay he would get the sarcophagus out of the pile of broken, looted coffins in the paupers' cave and stow it out of harm's way, in one of the other tombs in the labyrinth of tunnels they'd unearthed during the dig. He looked longingly at the right-hand tunnel again. Some of these passageways were quite steep, cut painstakingly by hand into the limestone bedrock by long-gone labourers. If he just let his burden slide downhill, there was every chance it would gather momentum and get away from him. Then it might collide with some solid object and smash into a million splinters.

No, he'd have to go up. 'Jay,' he groaned, 'it's pitch black. Nobody would see you here anyway. Couldn't you help me now?'

But he was talking to himself. As arranged (or rather, as ordered), while Albie moved the crucial evidence, Jay was making a great show of himself at the Oasis Orchid, ensuring that he was seen. And talking to that new dancer, Diselda, if Albie's suspicions were correct. Well, she was rather dazzling. Could hardly blame the chap for that.

So here he was, on his own, and he might as well get on with it. Thrusting the torch back under the edge of the coffin lid, Albie heaved on the foot end and turned it in the direction of the upper tunnel. Then he pushed.

No sooner had the torch entered the left-hand fork than the sign recurred – the sign that had shown Albie in the first place that this was not the tomb of a pauper. Beneath his palms the hacked-about, splintering wood of the coffin grew smooth. It was as if the coffin had just been moulded from fresh green twigs; it glowed and thrummed in his hands as if it were still growing, pulsating with life force.

At the head end, where the torch was wedged, the name on the sarcophagus began to glow. It was exactly as it had been when he had searched among the coffins, looking for the hawk that had blundered into the tomb and disappeared from sight, and later when he'd demonstrated for Lord Jay: a ghostly yellow light that grew increasingly more green and seemed to project the letters from the wood so they danced above the coffin like stars.

On both those occasions he'd let go abruptly, partly in shock, partly because he was aware that he had to keep this enormous discovery to himself. This time, in the inky depths of the tunnels, Albie held on, feeling the power surge from the new, green-tinged wood, up through his slender wrists and into his biceps. It felt like . . . like a blessing, he supposed. And it was definitely a sign that he was going the right way.

'Come along then, my dear Mr Skeleton,' he whispered. 'Let's get you somewhere comfortable.'

The name carved into the coffin lid blazed out in response. A familiar name. Ordinary, even. Only now Albie knew what it meant, since the boy had informed him what his own name stood for.

'ADJO,' he read aloud. Then he smiled as he recalled the translation. 'Treasure.'

Green, glowing . . . treasure. The resting place of Osiris. Here was confirmation indeed. Jay would be absolutely delighted with him. If he hadn't had one too many gin slings at the Oasis Orchid and passed out.

But suddenly the name echoed back at him, deafening in the confines of the tunnel. Adjo. ADJO. AADJOOO!

Albie jumped nearly out of his skin and snatched his hands away from the coffin. The glowing green aura remained. He prodded it quickly as if it was alive, but there was no change; removing his fingers as he had before did not cause the coffin to stop regenerating. Quite the opposite, in fact. As he looked on in terror and awe – wondering what on earth he had thought he was doing, shoving a godly coffin around the catacombs in the dark, all alone – a million green shoots sprang forth from the coffin, tendrils stretching around it, around the torch, towards Albie . . .

'Oh my word,' he said softly as the vines twisted around his legs and wrists and lifted him effortlessly on to the top of the sarcophagus. The fronds of green formed a fringe of legs around the bottom of the coffin, and Albie let out a low wail as the whole contraption scuttled up the tunnel like an enormous centipede, with Albie strapped to the top and completely unable to do anything to help himself. 'Jay . . .' he called out hopelessly, and then when nobody answered but the echoing walls, he screamed again: 'JAY!'

But once the echoes had died down, there was only quiet. The whisper of tender green shoots slithering along the tunnel floor. Ahead, the chime of running water. And what seemed to Albie the loudest noise of all — the unsteady pounding of his own heart.

9

Jack knew it wasn't a good time to ask his father to flex his aristocratic muscles and invite Prince William over to tea. Jack's facial bristles were already a centimetre long again, and he'd only got through the day at school by making sure he was sitting at the back of every class with his baseball hat and scarf on, refusing to take them off, and getting sent to the headmaster three or four times, where, needless to say, he failed to turn up.

Eventually, at about two p.m., Jack gave up. After staggering through drama, trying to make the scarf-and-hat get-up seem like some kind of method acting, so hot that he nearly passed out, he dashed out of the studio and Zipped back to Bone's. The valet was polishing shoes, his gaze a million miles away.

'Bone,' called Jack, getting his attention. 'Al-Bone, I'm dying here. I can't just keep leaving school or they'll start sending notes home and calling my parents in.' He tore the scarf off his head and saw Bone's eyes widen. 'If I Zip back now, could you forge me a note and turn up in the Daimler? Nobody will argue with that.'

Bone sighed, then nodded. Sure enough, once Jack had Zipped back to the school office and hung around fretting for a few minutes, the car appeared down the drive.

Jack watched its slow approach with mixed feelings. Normally he dreaded being caught anywhere near the enormous showy Daimler, as it marked him out from the other kids at Clearwell Comp more distinctly than anything. Anything except the head of a dog. Right now he needed all the distraction he could get. As he clambered into the back, Bone stalked up to the office with an embossed white envelope, complete with red wax seal, and handed it over to one of the dumb-founded school secretaries. With a sharp nod of the head, Bone retreated and joined Jack in the car.

'What did the note say?'

Bone opened his mouth and pointed.

'You told them? You told them I was doing the Opening of the Mouth ceremony? Bone, you idiot! They don't know I'm an Egyptian god. I can't . . .'

Bone shook his head, exasperated, grunting, 'Nggggg!'

'No?'

With deliberate exaggeration, Bone reclined his driver seat, clunked his jaw apart, then jabbed a fountain pen around his mouth, screaming at intervals.

'Oh. Dentist. Sorry, yeah, that makes sense.'

It made *more* sense, at any rate. Why it had been delivered in such a formal way, looking like a royal proclamation, Jack wasn't quite sure, but he didn't really feel that he was in a position to complain. Although Bone had righted his seat and driven away, he still looked like he could deliver a nasty jab in the eye with the nib of the pen if pushed further. Anyway, as Jack looked at the pen, clutched in Bone's left hand so it spun this way and that as he turned the steering wheel, he found the germ of an idea forming in the depths of his doggy mind.

'Are we going to the crypt?' he asked after a mile or two had gone by. Bone's mood didn't seem to have improved. He clearly had something on his mind, and Jack wanted to know what it was.

Bone muttered, 'Sir,' in a disconsolate fashion, and

turned off at the first left turning, heading to the back of the graveyard instead of to the main Lowmount Hall entrance. Despite its being midsummer, and mid-afternoon, there was a low bank of misty grey cloud sitting above the graveyard, and Jack felt his hackles rise as he got out of the car. Blackie and the other jackals were lying in the gateway, not quite meeting his eye, and he could see that they were on alert, watching out for something. They too were sensing the prevailing black mood, it seemed.

Once inside the crypt, it seemed a bit more cheer-ful, not least because all the candles were flickering brightly, and his great-grandparents were performing a ghostly cha-cha along the top of Granny Dazzle's sarcophagus. When Jack turned round, Bone had once more transformed into Albie and was nervously chewing the end of his slender moustache as he stared at the dancing duo.

'Great, now you can speak, Albert Bone Corn-thwaite,' said Jack, waving hello to the ghosts.

'It's Albert *Bartholomew* Cornthwaite, actually,' said Albie snootily.

Jack ignored him. If he rose to the bait every time someone started something at the moment, he'd always be in an argument. 'So what was going on with my dad this morning?'

The transparent forms of the ghosts stopped dancing, and Albie gave a nervous cough. 'I'd rather not say.'

'But . . . but I want to know,' said Jack.

Albie glared at him, and then his eyes flicked around the crypt. He seemed extremely jittery. 'I do not have to tell you everything,' he said finally. 'Unless you order me to, of course – seeing as I'm just a servant, by dint of my lowly birth, and, as if that wasn't bad enough, seeing as I'm actually cursed to do your family's bidding for ever and a day.'

'Ah.' Now Jack understood the bitter tone. Of course he did – his father could bring out that kind of reaction in a saint. The current Lord Bootle-Cadogan had been laying down the law and had offended Al-Bone. There was still another layer of tension, though, that he didn't quite follow. Only when he saw Albie's eyes flash once again to the ghosts who were now embracing on top of the portmanteau did he get an inkling of what it might be. Was Al-Bone . . . jealous? Envious of Jay and Diselda's relationship? If so, he needed them out of the way.

'Granny Dazzle, Grandpa Jay, was there anything you needed right now? Albie's going to help me with some history homework. You know what a mega-brain he is.'

Looking disappointed, the ghosts shook their heads, rattling the contents of the portmanteau, and then spun faster and faster in a vortex until they disappeared.

'There. Gone. Now will you tell me?'

For a long moment it looked as though Albie was going to refuse to say anything at all. Once he'd opened his mouth, however, it poured out in a thick, embittered stream, so that Jack couldn't get a word in.

'He's a lovely man, your father,' started Albie, with an expression that said Lord Bootle-Cadogan was anything but lovely. 'Started by telling me that I hadn't cleaned the Daimler properly, and he wasn't sure what he was employing me for if I couldn't do even the most basic of tasks properly. Then he reminded me just how long I'd been with the family and enjoying – how did he put it? – free board and lodging in a beautiful cottage that could have made them a fortune on the open market. And obviously as Bone I couldn't interrupt him and tell him that I was actually employed as an archaeologist by his grandfather and made one of the most important discoveries of the modern age myself, yes, me, myself, and that I was never actually a servant, at least not until I turned up here with my memory and body blown apart and was treated with kindness and dignity by Lady Diselda.'

To Jack's horror, a fat tear trickled out from beneath his friend's little round spectacles. Albie had told him the story of how he had arrived at Lowmount after he and Lord Jay had been cursed by Seth. His Lordship had died, and the force of the god's power had flayed Albie's skin and made him lose his memory completely. It was only by a massive stroke of luck that he had managed to find his way back to Lowmount and to Lord Jay's beloved wife, who took him in and treated him like family.

'No, I couldn't interrupt him,' continued Albie in a strangled tone, 'so I just had to stand there like a . . . like a servant, Jack, which is all I am, all I ever became . . . while your wonderful father told me I'd better forget all claims to this back-pay nonsense or I'd be out on my ear. Furthermore, he expects me to get the other servants – I mean, staff – to do the same.

He threatened me. Told me I'd lose my home. The only home I've known for nearly a century. Never a day's pay, Jack! I've never had a day's pay, not since I was an honest undertaker. There! There, I've told you! And now you can throw me out as well!'

Jack couldn't think of a thing to say. How awful. How completely awful. He could hardly believe that his own flesh and blood would be capable of such cruel, heartless behaviour.

'What do you mean, I can throw you out as well?' he asked suddenly. 'I'd never do that. You're my friend, Albie, and you were Granny Dazzle's friend when she was terribly lonely, and you were Jay's right-hand man, his very best friend. You helped him find the resting place of Osiris, for Pete's sake. You're practically family, Albie, and the only person who thinks anything other than that is my stupid father. And you have to admit, he is very, very stupid.'

Albie sniffed quietly. 'I suppose he is a tiny bit stupid,' he said in a small voice.

'Hey, you can do better than that. He's a complete idiot.'

'Maybe an idiot sometimes. All right, most of the time.' Allowing himself a tiny smile, Albie finished:

'Actually, I've always considered him an utter buffoon.'

'Exactly!' Jack smiled back uncertainly. Was it a good thing to be calling your own father 'an utter buffoon'? Probably not, and his father did have the occasional moment when he seemed a bit more human, so he wasn't one-hundred-per-cent buffoon. But mostly . . . well, yes, it had to said. And Albie had visibly cheered up.

He thumped him in the arm. 'Would you rather . . . be eaten by Seth or patronized by my father?'

'Eaten by Seth,' said Albie with barely a moment's thought. 'His breath's better.'

'It's all that cheese my father eats,' said Jack. 'And the red wine.'

'I've got one for you,' said Albie. 'Would you rather . . . be a servant or be a Bootle-Cadogan?'

'Oh.' That was a hard one. Too hard by far. And a little unfair. 'I can't answer that one. That's saying all servants are the same, and all Bootle-Cadogans are the same.'

'Maybe they are,' said Albie.

They were back on dangerous ground. Either Seth's

nasty influence was getting stronger or Albie hadn't actually cheered up that much at all. Jack shook his head. 'I'm not, Albie, I promise you. I'm not the same. I'll prove it to you.'

Albie stared at him as if he really wanted to believe it, but just as Jack was about to speak the door from the museum tunnel crashed open, and Ozzy and Ice spirited themselves into the crypt, a whirling dervish of green, ice-white and blue.

Jack knew instantly what that meant. 'He's here?'

'N-not here, b-but nearby,' stammered Ice, eyes glinting fearfully.

'Nearby he is,' said Ozzy. 'We were in the museum listening to your transmitter of the waves and the people suddenly were screaming. Screaming about a wild boar.'

'It could actually *be* a wild boar,' said Albie quickly. 'I saw one once, in the woods nearby.'

'No, this is the type of terror that only Seth can induce,' said Ozzy, turning such a pale green he looked as if he was about to vomit.

Ice beckoned to them. 'Come. You hear too.'

In no time they had rushed along the corridor to

the museum. Jack stumbled out through the Eye of Horus door, half expecting the room to be in disarray again. Everything was much as it should be, however, and it looked as though Ozzy and Ice had been having a pleasant afternoon stretched out on the camp beds listening to the cricket on the radio which sat on a camp stool between them. The *radio*. 'Ah, so that's the transmitter of the waves.'

'People on their bicycles in the forest have been attacked by a ferocious pig,' announced Ozzy in a formal voice like a newsreader.

'Attacked they have been,' confirmed Ice, twiddling the knob on the radio to get better reception.

As they all sat down on the camp beds, Ozzy and Ice on one side and Bone and Jack on the other, the cricket commentary was interrupted by a newsflash. As the reporter updated listeners on the wild-boar attack at a local holiday camp, they could hear a voice in the background that sounded oddly familiar to Jack. 'Ladies . . . and gentlemmmm, there is no need for alarm. The police have been . . . called and are on their way. Please return . . . to your cabins . . . and await further notice. I repeat, there is no need for aaal . . .'

'Alarm,' they all said together. The poor man sounded desperately short of breath, and also as if there was *every* need for alarm. He was clearly petrified.

Jack stood up. 'Ozzy'n'Ice, Ice'n'Ozzy, I think you should contact Minty and then get yourselves to the crypt. You're probably safest there, and maybe the ghosts can help if there's any trouble.'

'What shall I do, O master?' sighed Bone with a grovelling bow.

Jack didn't have time for this any more. 'Firstly, get over yourself. And secondly, grab your snakey stick or anything you might need from the ceremonial suitcase. You can give something evil a good crack with it.'

'It is a *naboot*,' said Ozzy, 'for ceremonial purposes – not for *Tahtib*.'

'It's not a what for what?' Whatever it was or wasn't, Jack noticed that Bone was holding the sinister-looking hollow staff pretty close as he paced the museum.

Ozzy explained. 'You have seen this *asa* used in our ceremonies, Jack. It is a ceremonial object, not a fighting stick as used in the ancient and contemporary

Egyptian martial art of *Tahtib*.'

'Well, we'll see exactly what it's good for soon. You and I, Al-Bone my *friend* –' and Jack emphasized the word – 'are going on a pig hunt.'

10

They left the museum. Jack was itching to run but had to slow to allow Bone's older body to get to the Daimler. Jack had never tried to Zip another person, but he had done it with the car, so he knew that that way they could get to their destination together at the same speed that he could get there himself.

Bone automatically opened the door for Jack, but Jack pushed him gently around to his own door and jumped into the passenger seat. As soon as Bone had strapped on his seat belt, Jack grabbed the steering wheel. 'We're heading to that new holiday park,' he said. 'Hold on. I'm driving.'

Then he pictured the little car park he'd stood near while salivating over the sausages just the previous evening. The image settled into his mind's eye, and with a lurch they were off, the car whooshing straight through the gravestones, the crypt door, Granny Dazzle's tomb and the edge of the little tunnel to the museum.

'Ooops, sorry,' said Jack.

Bone glared at him as he corrected the steering wheel with a wizened hand, and suddenly they Zipped off in a different direction, out through the trickle of cottages around the edges of Lowmount village, through one or two of the living rooms he'd passed through the other evening – since it was earlier in the day, a couple of old ladies watching Oprah and a young mum having an afternoon nap with her baby got rather a surprise – and straight across the black tarmac sheen of the M4 motorway and the straggle of caravans that were heading in both directions. They left a couple of them still wavering in their wake as they ploughed across some nearby fields and then entered the bracken and ferns that marked the edge of the forest.

'Nearly there!' called Jack cheerfully. Bone's head was pushed back against the seat, and his eyes were firmly shut; whether it was the G-forces or just Bone's way of avoiding locking eyes with startled pensioners Jack didn't know, but he was pretty sure that Bone was perilously close to throwing up.

But they really were almost there. As a couple of sturdy sycamore trees appeared to pass through the steering column of the car and straight through Bone's body, Jack felt the tighten-then-release sensation in his gut that heralded the end of a Zip journey. The car park was just ahead of them as they slowed. Unfortunately he hadn't visualized a parking space, as such, so they were just about to smash into a well-loved Land Rover when suddenly the brakes were slammed on. They screeched to a halt with the bumpers scraping.

Jack smiled apologetically as Bone straightened up. 'It's rather dark here, for mid-June at four in the afternoon.'

They got out of the car slowly. There was something about the dim light and swirling floor of the forest that made Jack slightly nervous. He stood taller and sniffed the air. Taller was quite a lot taller, now that he was becoming more Doghead and less boy, and he could sniff out a variety of people and their various emotions. The overriding aroma was musky and unpleasant. 'Fear,' growled Jack. 'Everyone's frightened. Come on. Let's go.'

Leaving the car park behind, they trudged across an area of low ferns and bushes towards the chalets. A few lights peeked out through the trees, and beyond there was a glint of something large and shiny. An office building? Jack made a mental note of it; it might be where to find the manager who was putting out those raspy messages over the intercom.

Bone pointed down the path ahead, gesturing for Jack to go first.

'Scared?'

'No. Blind,' said the look on Bone's face.

'That's all right. I don't mind going first.' Jack trotted past Bone and peered ahead into the gloom. It really was strangely dark, more like dusk than late afternoon. The trees swished around them, stirred by a strengthening breeze, and Jack began to feel more than ever that something very peculiar was going on. 'The branches of the trees, Al-Bone. Look.'

'Si-ir,' groaned Bone, frustrated, pointing once again to his weak violet eyes.

It was hard to put into words. 'They don't look like ordinary branches. They're more like . . . snakes.'

'O Rerek,' bleated Bone mournfully. It sounded like a swear word.

No sooner had the sigh left Bone's lips than the skies above them turned black. Jack tried to see what was happening, only to find that the ominous block of colour was not sky at all – it was the branches of

97

the trees, twisted away and off the trunks, mutating into glimmering enormous black snakes of every species and size, raining down on them and snapping, coiling, intent on the kill.

'Run!' screamed Jack, flinging an inky black asp off his arm as another slid down the back of his shirt.

Aware that Bone was more vulnerable than he was, Jack resisted Zipping away and tried not to recoil as he stepped on a writhing carpet of snakes underfoot. As fast as he stripped them away from his body, they reappeared, dropping down on him, some slamming into him as if they'd been fired from a gun. Sure enough, when he found a chink of light that enabled him to look up at the trees, he saw that the branches were renewing themselves on the trunks, sprouting from the thick wood like black extruded Play-Doh, coursing through the air like arrows from a bow. This was definitely Seth's work.

'Sir!' Bone clutched at his shoulder and Jack let out a shout, closing his jaws again rapidly when he realized a snake was slithering down over his forehead and heading for his mouth.

Bone was fighting madly with his stick, his impression of a martial-arts expert admirable for someone who professed to have no knowledge of it. The stick flailed madly in a whirling figure-of-eight, and minced snakes flew outwards as if in a blender without a lid. Jack snatched a snake that was trying to coil itself around Bone's ankles and caught a blinding clunk in the temple from the stick.

'I'll try to Zip us out of here!' Jack screamed. Surely he'd be able to Zip them both if he could move a whole car. There were far too many of the creatures to fight off, particularly as new ones were being born as fast as old ones died. But just as Jack was about to get hold of Albie's shoulder and picture the safety of the Daimler, he heard a distant sound that turned him cold.

'We can't go,' he shouted, snapping a snake in half with his canine jaws and casting the two parts aside. 'I just heard a kid crying.'

It sounded like the boy he'd heard exclaiming over his hot dog the other night. People who had no chance of fighting this evil were in grave danger – right here. 'We have to go and help.'

Bone sighed, then spun round so his back was in view. Jack knew what he meant. 'Back to back. You lead.' It was a way to be as protected as possible while still allowing Jack's better senses to guide them forward.

They stood shoulder to shoulder and quickly linked their arms together so they wouldn't get separated. Then in a pair they lunged through the forest towards the chalets, kicking and shoving and occasionally passing the stick over their heads to each other as they knocked snake after snake back into the darkness.

'There's one going up your trouser leg, I can't get it,' squeaked Jack.

In a flash, Bone pointed the head of the stick at the tail of the snake and screamed something unintelligible, then yelled again as the snake wriggled further up his leg. Diving to the ground, Bone frantically reached into his pocket for his notepad and scribbled a note to Jack.

'"Say this,"' Jack read. 'OK.' As Bone pointed the stick at the snake again, Jack intoned: '"He will be one proscribed; he will be one who eats himself!"'

Jack glanced down just as the snake tumbled on to Albie's shoe, grabbed its own tail in its mouth and proceeded to devour itself until the stubby head tumbled to the ground, dead. 'Eww. That was gross.'

Bone looked away in disgust.

'Never mind. We made it,' said Jack.

They had come through the thicket of trees, and were now standing at the edge of one of the small gravelled areas that acted as a garden for its chalet. As the trees had run out, so had the snakes, and now it appeared almost as a normal holiday park, though it was noticeable that none of the barbecues was being used and the doors and windows were closed. Instead, families sat huddled on their couches, and through the windows Jack could see some parents feverishly packing suitcases. And there was the crying again. He followed the sound in his long loping stride.

Remembering his odd appearance, Jack halted in his tracks. He really wanted to check the boy was all right, but it was going to be difficult without terrifying him. 'Bone, could you be official? Check the wood-work or something?'

In response, Bone raised an eyebrow, straightened his jacket and headed towards the back door of the nearest chalet. As he rapped smartly, Jack wedged himself behind the barbecue so that only his head was sticking out.

'Sir,' said Bone to the man who appeared at the back door. He shook the startled man's hand, then pulled a piece of paper from his pocket and mimed 'checking things' at him. Spotting Jack at knee level, Bone patted his head awkwardly.

The man peered behind Bone and then nodded to Jack. 'Keep your dog close, if you know what's good for you,' he said darkly. 'This place is possessed. Snakes all over the decking this morning there were, and then this afternoon my boy was sitting out here and a wild pig lunged at him out of nowhere – nowhere! Lucky he got through the dog flap in time. And now this unnatural darkness. It's June! I paid good money for this. Paid!'

As he went on to Bone about his disgust at not getting the weather or snake-free environment that one would expect for what he'd paid, Jack, having made sure the man was fully occupied, pictured the little boy with the ketchup-and-mustard combo running down his chin. *Zoom!* Without the man noticing anything, Jack had Zipped sideways through the kitchen wall, across the bathroom and into the wardrobe in the boy's room. Peeking out, Jack saw the boy sitting on the top bunk, cuddling a toy rabbit.

Jack was about to burst out of the cupboard when he remembered what he looked like. The boy had already had one horrible attack today – he didn't need another hairy beast leaping out at him now. Suddenly he had a brainwave. With his eyes firmly on the bottom bunk, he allowed himself to Zip effortlessly to the bed below the boy.

He channelled his voice into a rabbit-like squeak and spoke upward through the metal slats of the bed above. 'Hello, I'm your rabbit.'

'Buttons!' screeched the boy. 'Argghghg!'

'Please don't . . . don't scream,' squeaked Jack quickly. Sensitive hearing could sometimes be a bit of a pain. 'Buttons is here to help. And rabbits have big, big ears that hurt a lot when you scream. You don't want to hurt wickle Buttons, do you? You've done enough screaming today, haven't you?'

'Ye-es,' came the tentative reply. 'It was scary.'

'Tell Buttons all about it,' said Jack. 'After you tell me your name.'

'Jo-Jo-Joseph. It was ho-horrible,' said the boy, about to cry again. 'The nasty pig jumped out of the trees and it was going to EAT me, and I said, NO, nasty pig, and then it . . . it laughed at me and it said, You're too SMALL for me, but still you'd better RUN, so I did run, I did, I got straight through the doggy flap.' The boy paused. 'He didn't sound like you, Buttons; he had a horrid growly voice.'

'Well, he's a horrid nasty pig and not a nice fwendly wabbit like me,' said Jack. 'And where did the nasty pig go after that?'

'I fink it went to the wave pool.'

Jack hesitated. 'For a . . . swim?'

'I don't know, Buttons. He was just roaring like a lion.'

Jack knew all about roaring. 'Was he saying, "RAAAAAAAAaaa?" Like that?'

'Yes!'

'All right,' said Jack. 'You've been a very good boy. Why don't you go to sleep now?'

'I haven't had my tea yet.'

Ah yes. It was only just past four o'clock. It was so dark outside it could have been much later in the evening. 'Oh. Right. Well, Buttons will look after you from now on, so don't you be fwightened. Just go and see Mummy and Daddy and it will all be fine.'

'Thank you, Buttons! Are you going to talk to me every day now?'

Argh! How disappointing was that going to be?! Think, Jack, think, he told himself. Then: 'No, Buttons only ever needs to talk to you when you've been horribly fwightened, and you're never going to be scared like that again. Never. OK?' Genius.

'OK,' said the small voice above his head. 'Bye, Buttons.'

As Jack Zipped back to behind the barbecue, he couldn't help feeling rather proud of himself. Doghead, God of the Dead and protector of small boys. It was quite a neat job.

Bone cast his eyes down quickly and registered that Jack was back. 'Sir,' he said with what passed for a smile in Bone-world. He almost winked matily, then simply said, 'Sir,' again, and pointed to the little sign-post that said 'Manager'.

The man tutted. 'You'd better be quick. Never known anyone so short of breath,' he said as he closed the door.

Jack pulled Bone to the side of the chalet. 'Pig-face wasn't attacking the boy; he was saying, "Ra," and heading to the wave pool. Which is where we need to go now.'

Bone's lugubrious face grew even longer. He pointed

through the gaps in the chalets, beyond another few rows of the little huts, to the distant gleaming roof.

Between them and it lay a ring of trees as thick as the forest behind. The trees appeared to be different to the tall, spiky firs that had spewed out the snakes, but Jack still didn't fancy it.

'Wow! How many snakes would that be? We'll have to come back with reinforcements,' he said. 'And maybe in daylight.'

But as it was supposed to be daylight right at that moment, when they were heading towards the longest day of the year, there was no saying how much Seth had brought forward the darkest, darkest night.

11

'There's something very spooky about that forest,' said Jack.

Bone shrugged, unable to say very much. However, there wasn't terribly much that needed to be said at this stage: now they were heading away from the forest, the gloom and the mood were lifting, not to the level they should be for a midsummer day, but certainly brighter than the last hour or so. In fact, it was almost pleasant driving through the countryside in the early evening, with the white-flowered hedgerows brushing against the car and the birds gathering in evensong. Jack hardly wanted to go inside, especially into a cold and dingy crypt, but the events at the holiday park had shown that there was much to be done.

True to form, Bone became Albie again as they entered the family mausoleum. 'I'm sure this changing can't be good for me,' he grumbled, rubbing his arms.

'I'd swear my arthritis is getting worse when I'm Bone.'

'You're moaning again! What is going on with everybody?' Jack slapped him on the back. 'Look at it this way: would you rather be just Bone without arthritis, or Albie sometimes and Bone sometimes with a bit of arthritis?'

'I suppose you're right,' said Albie, crossing over to the portmanteau. 'Has someone been ransacking this, do you think?'

There was stuff all over the floor. Ceremonial robes lay draped across the stone altar steps, and all the accoutrements they used in the Opening of the Mouth ritual had been scattered across the crypt, exposing a second layer of tiny shelves in the portmanteau, which contained row upon row of strangely shaped bottles and boxes.

Jack picked up the Feather of Ma'at, which used to be hidden in Granny Dazzle's headdress but had now wafted across the crypt and was in grave danger of being set alight by one of the night lights flickering along the walls. 'That was close. Is anything missing?'

'We won't know until we put everything back. I'll start with the *naboot*.' As Albie clicked his snake stick back into position, there was a thickening of the air above his head and then an odd lick of flame that sprang out of nowhere. The portmanteau shuddered as Albie yelled, 'It's alive!'

'No, it's the great-grands,' said Jack. 'I can just about see Lord Jay's moustache, and Granny Dazzle's dancing shoes, although they're a bit shady apart from that. Oh, who's that?'

There was somebody else, or rather some non-body else with them, floating off to one side. Jack couldn't quite make it out, sensing rather than seeing a tall figure with an imposing presence and an energy that felt very like Lord Jay's. And like his father's, when he considered it. It wasn't until he peered straight up into the curve of the roof and saw a spectral pair of peculiarly long ear lobes (a family trait he'd been unfortunate enough to inherit) that he realized who it was. 'Ah, Grandpa Johnnie! Hello there.'

'Your great-grandparents are bringing in reinforcements,' said Albie a trifle stiffly.

Granny Dazzle and Lord Jay danced around on the portmanteau to make it shake, while Jack's grandfather nodded, his ghostly ear lobes flapping gently. Albie was right.

'You're getting wispier each time I see you,' said Jack. 'Johnnie, you're almost completely transparent. Is this all because of Seth's reappearance too?'

There was more suitcase-shaking and ear-flapping. They were on the right track.

'And there's something in here that will help deal with it – make you less see-through, and maybe . . . make everyone less miserable?'

The portmanteau rattled in response, although Jack couldn't help but notice that the movement was not as effective as the hanger-swishing in the wardrobe had been. 'They're losing their powers,' he said softly to Albie.

Albie sniffed, and Jack could almost swear that he saw his friend pull a face at Ear-lobe Johnnie. 'Maybe it's time.'

'How can you say that? This was your friend, Al-Bone. I know you've got your bandages in a knot about this whole back-pay thing,' said Jack, suddenly cross with Albie, 'but don't go accusing us all of being like my father.'

Albie merely shrugged.

Jack didn't like the look on his face, but he thought he understood. 'This isn't us, Albie. It's this mad bad mood that the porky one is putting us in. Let's just focus on what we have to do to get rid of him. I think it helps to be doing something.' Anything instead of arguing, he wanted to add, but he could see that Albie was backing down a little and decided not to push it.

He looked up at his wispy ancestors. 'Right, we're going to hold things up and you have to give us a sign if it's the item you're looking for.'

He couldn't help sniggering. Dressed in their evening finery, they looked like a panel of judges on *Strictly Come Dancing*, and Jack would have loved to give them scorecards to hold up. But holding on to anything seemed to be beyond them right now, so he settled for: 'Put out a candle if it's wrong, and shake the portmanteau if it's right.'

Albie retrieved his martial-arts stick and held it up, and instantly one of the little candle flames disappeared, snuffed out by Johnnie's ghostly foot. It was Jack's turn; fairly sure now that it wasn't any of the items they'd used before in the ceremonies, he picked out a bottle labelled 'Sheep's Eyeballs' and waved it around. Out went another candle.

They went along the rows of vials, finding it harder

and harder to read the labels as more candles were extinguished, until they were going by feel as much as anything. 'This wasn't such a good plan,' said Jack to Albie, his arm weary from holding bottle after bottle up close enough for the ghosts to see. 'If the next two aren't right, we'll be completely in the dark.'

'Good job I'm here then,' said a voice in the darkness. A large altar candle burst into flame, and there stood Minty, blowing on the end of her finger as if she'd just fired a pistol.

'Yes, light them all,' said Jack, relieved.

'What's the magic word?'

'Quickly!'

'Please,' interjected Albie before Minty set fire to Jack's ears instead.

When the candles were all relit, Jack was surprised to see Ozzy and Ice were also in the crypt. 'Hello, you two, I didn't hear you come in!'

'Ozzy is sad. We did not find his missing crown,' said Ice.

'Find it we did not.'

'We don't really know where to start looking,' said Minty. 'Where would you stash a missing crown?'

Jack shrugged. 'The Tower of London?'

'No, that's a royal crown,' said Albie. 'This is part of Ozzy's body, for goodness sake. It's just as likely to be in a jar in China as in the Tower of London.'

The conversation seemed to interest the ghosts greatly – candles suddenly guttered and fizzed, and the portmanteau was practically dancing on its own. 'Is the missing crown in here?' asked Jack excitedly.

There was a small pause while the ghosts conferred, then a slight rattle of the trunk was accompanied by two candles going out. 'What does that mean? It either is or it isn't,' said Jack.

Albie twisted the ends of his moustache, which was a sure sign that he was thinking. 'Not necessarily, Jack. Remember the Ancient Egyptians were very fond of symbolism, so that items might be used that would represent something, like the *shabtis* that were used in coffins to represent the servants one would have in the afterlife.'

Granny Dazzle and Jay appeared to like that. They twirled and dipped in a tango above their heads. 'OK, so there's something still in this trunk which will . . . stand in for Ozzy's head, is that right?' Jack peered up at the shimmering outlines of his ancestors.

Definitely. All three were jumping up and down in thin air.

'Well, there are only two things left.' Grabbing a candle, Jack pressed his long nose up to the shelves. Neither item looked anything like a bit of a skull – there was a box made of thick card with 'Camel Dung' inscribed in scribbly writing on the side, and then what looked like perfume, in a tiny bottle with a tall spiky top made of crystal. That one had to be Granny Dazzle's, so Jack opened the cardboard box and tipped the camel dung on to his hand. 'Oh, it could be a piece of skull. It looks a bit like matted hair. Ozzy, do you recognize it?'

Ozzy shook his head mournfully, and at the same moment half a dozen candles went out at once.

'Not that then,' said Jack. 'So it has to be this.'

Being careful not to drop it, Jack took hold of the perfume bottle. The container itself was just a little ball of glass with an amber liquid sloshing around inside it, and didn't appear very remarkable at all. The stopper was more spectacular – a tall triangle of glass that was shaved away on all sides like a diamond, so that when Jack held it up to the light the candle flames were magnified and fiery colours shot around the room.

The ghosts went wild, shimmying the portmanteau so hard that the noise was like a round of applause, and Jack stared at the vial.

'This has to be some amazing liquid. I don't know what to do with it though,' he said. 'Albie, any ideas?'

Albie took it from him gently and studied it with an expression almost of tenderness. 'I'm not sure. It could be a special embalming oil that was used to preserve the missing piece of Osiris. Or perhaps some sort of anointing liquid.' He looked up at Jack. 'I suppose there's only one way to find out.'

They both glanced over at Ozzy, who paled to a green that was almost yellow but then sat himself with dignity on the edge of the altar. 'We will try it,' he said.

'Try it we will,' said Ice, hovering anxiously nearby.

Jack jumped up on to the altar and stood behind Ozzy, holding out a hand for the bottle. The view from up here wasn't especially pretty. He could see straight down between the jagged edges of the hole in Ozzy's crown and was half-expecting to glimpse a wobbly brain pulsing away in there. There was nothing like that, however – just a shimmering white lining, as if he was staring down into a split coconut.

'No brain, Jack; we take it out in mummification,' said Albie quickly, reading his thoughts.

'So what do I do? Pour this into the hole?' That had to hurt, even for a god without a brain.

Nobody seemed to have any better ideas, and the ghostly grandparents were struggling to get their point of view across, so Jack carefully removed the stopper, which was as long as his hand. Passing it to Albie, he held the little bottle over Ozzy's head and tipped it, ready to pour . . .

Every candle in the room went out.

'Oi!' shouted Jack. 'I can't see what I'm doing! We can't waste this stuff.'

Had Seth arrived? Around Jack people and gods were scrabbling around in the dark, trying to find their footing and colliding with tombs and each other. Finally Minty managed to find a stub of candle and ignite it, then used it to go from candle to candle, illuminating the room. Jack had never appreciated just how much they relied on the candles to see. 'Must talk to my parents about getting some spots put in,' he said.

'That will go down well,' said Albie sardonically. 'More expense, bigger bills, and so on and so forth . . .'

He had a point. 'Anyway,' said Jack, 'who put the candles out?'

The ghosts above his head wavered around for a moment.

'You?'

The portmanteau rattled. Yes.

'So I shouldn't go dropping this stuff into Ozzy's head?'

Pfff. All the night lights along the top of Granny Dazzle's tomb went out. Apparently not.

It was hopeless. What was he supposed to do? Jack could only think about how hungry he was, and how he couldn't possibly go to dinner with a dog's head, as the atmosphere of depression descended once again in the crypt.

12

After a few minutes of trotting along the passageway, ducking to avoid being concussed by the low tunnel roof, Albie settled in for the ride. It felt as though he were loafing along on the back of a big, friendly Great Dane, albeit a green one bristling with leaves and springtime shoots. It was fairly galloping now, lunging friskily towards the distant sound of running water.

'You're completely missing out, Lord Jay, dear boy,' he hiccuped softly as they bounced along, mimicking his friend's aristocratic tones. His own language was much plainer, more suited to his working-class origins, but Albie couldn't help but notice that being 'posh' opened far more doors than being a lowly undertaker.

Anyway, it was true. Jay would have loved this. It was far more his cup of tea than Albie's — adventures and mysteries, following whims and life's weird and wonderful rolls of the dice. He'd funded the whole trip, after all, especially to seek out Osiris's resting place, and now he wasn't here to experience this. With his hands caught up in slender green vines, unable to reach for his pencil and notebook, Albie made mental notes of what was happening, so he could pass on every detail when he found Jay in the morning. It was a good way to keep calm.

'Um . . . oh, oh, mind the roof. Um . . . Adjo – the name is glowing again. Osiris must like it, or something. These tendrils appear to be . . . not olive or palm or even a vine . . . perhaps tamarind? Argh! What was that? Snake! Calm down, Albie. All right. We're following the sound of water – well, that would make sense, since Osiris would need it to make the vegetation grow and so on. Still going uphill though. Don't like it. No. That's strange, I wonder . . . Ah!'

His shout combined sudden comprehension with complete surprise, as the passageway finished abruptly and the coffin sprang forward on its little green legs on to a large, smooth stepping stone at the edge of an enormous underground lake.

Albie held on grimly as the sarcophagus bounded along joyfully, launching itself from stone to stone as it made its way towards the centre of the vast cavern they had come to. When he saw what they were heading for, he gasped.

This was no ordinary underground lake. Now that he could see it properly, glistening with diamond intensity as the water sparkled and danced around him, Albie realized it was almost like the ornamental fountain in the grounds at Lowmount, with one central jet of water shooting straight upward and four smaller jets spurting up at equal intervals around it. At Lowmount, however, the water was ejected from the mouth of a rather ugly mermaid statue and the blowholes of the four dolphins that flanked her. Here, the water was more like one of the geothermal geysers in America and New Zealand that Albie had read about, surging straight up for forty or fifty feet as if shot from a cannon, with four smaller spouts at each of the compass points. 'The Children of Horus,' squeaked Albie. All the water emanated from an enormous glistening jade statue of Osiris, with plaited beard, flail and crook, and a calm, munificent Mona Lisa smile across his noble features.

'Glory be,' breathed Albie. It was glorious indeed – an underground spring bursting forth from the limestone bedrock, forced up through the statue and carving out the walls of the beautiful cathedral-sized cavern; walls from which vines tumbled, lush with fruit and tropical flowers, their vibrant emerald leaves kissing the surface of the pool into which the fountain gushed and thundered.

The bounding coffin had reached the last stepping stone before the round central plinth on which the statue rested. Between them and the centre of the cavern stretched a churning expanse of water – well over a hundred yards, by Albie's estimation. Just as he was wondering how high the coffin would have to jump to cross this distance, he sensed something changing in the sarcophagus beneath him. The twiggy legs on which they'd been scampering and jumping were extending again; at the edge of the stepping stone the front legs slid into the water and appeared again moments later with more vegetation clamped in their coils. 'Reeds,' whispered Albie. 'They're making a barque.'

Sure enough, the tendrils worked like many slender hands, binding the papyrus reeds into sheaves and then drawing them in around the coffin. In seconds the sarcophagus was sitting on a long, narrow platform of woven papyrus that formed an Ancient Egyptian ceremonial boat, ready to take to the water to transport the coffin, its contents, and its living passenger, across the final stretch of water to the statue island.

It was only then that Albie realized the full extent of what was happening. Osiris's final resting place was not the coffin at all. It was across the water, there in the fountain of life in the centre of the cavern. And he, lowly Albert Cornthwaite, was the first to stumble across – no, to be transported to – this legendary centre of life and renewal.

'Abydos.' He whispered the name of the legendary city reverently, as the barque slid into the choppy waters and edged its way towards the fountain. 'I've found the heart of Abydos!'

As if to confirm it, the barque surged forward, and Albie held on for dear life.

13

With Seth on the warpath it seemed as if Doghead was here to stay – Jack was concerned to discover that he was more dog than boy at the moment, even when he wasn't in the crypt. This meant that he had to keep a low profile, and the only way he was able to avoid his parents was by camping out, more or less full-time, at Bone's cottage. It also killed two birds with one stone, as Jack was very careful to make sure that Bone overheard the telephone conversation he had with his mother.

'Mum, it's me,' he said loudly. 'Do you know what Father has been saying to Bone?'

'Oh, I dread to think,' came the reply.

'He's been telling him to forget all claims to his back pay, and to make all the other . . . um . . . working guys do the same, or he'll be turfed out of his cottage. It's disgusting, Mum. Bone never expected any pay in the first place, but for Dad to blackmail

123

him by threatening him with the loss of his home is just awful.'

His mother let out a long sigh. 'I know, Jack. But what can we do?'

Spotting in the mirror that Bone was trying his hardest not to overhear and was about to leave the room, Jack raised his voice a notch. 'Well, we can't do nothing. So I've decided on a course of action. I'm going to stage a sit-in.'

'A sit-in?'

'Yes,' said Jack firmly. 'I'm going to stay here at Bone's until he comes to his senses – Dad, I mean, not Bone. If Dad turns up to chuck Bone out, he'll have to chuck me out too.'

There was a long silence, which he hoped might end with resigned agreement from his mother. Then the phone came alive in his hand. 'Jack Algernon Bootle-Cadogan, do not leave me here on my own to deal with your father! He's completely unreasonable. Won't listen to sense. Won't try to get a loan to just sort out the blessed back pay and let us get on with our lives. Won't ever forget that he's a lord of the realm, as if that matters one jot these days. We're as outdated as the royal family.'

124

Which reminded him. 'Oh. Do you think you could invite Prince William to tea on the twenty-first? It's his birthday.'

'No, Jack,' said his mother frostily, 'I do not. Now, I will see you in the dining room at eight o'clock for dinner. If you're going to be sleeping in the cottage, then the least I expect is a daily visit.'

Jack thought quickly. His mother was actually being quite accommodating, and he didn't want to go and ruin it. 'OK,' he said slowly. 'But only if you try to save money on the power bill by having it just candle-lit. And not many candles, because they're expensive too.'

His mother agreed, only the tiniest bit reluctantly, and he popped the phone back on Bone's hall table. He was free. Wow. He was going to be living in a normal little cottage, with only one TV set, and one of everything really, and no servants and . . . well, OK, Bone was still a servant *technically*, but more than that, he was Jack's buddy. If only he could be Albie more of the time, they could have a riot.

Bone installed him in the spare bedroom under the eaves, which was approximately the size of Granny Dazzle's walk-in closet and which Jack adored from the outset. Then he drove them over to the Hall, and as Jack padded his way down the hall to the dining room, wearing a hoody that made it impossible to see his face, canine or otherwise, Bone ambled off to get Jack's uniform and school bag, ready for his sit-in time.

The dining room was only dimly illuminated when he pushed open the door, much to his relief. And the table was so long that, when he sat down in the middle, his parents were far away from him at the distant ends and could hardly see him at all.

'What's that ridiculous thing you're wearing? Take your hat off at the table,' barked his father.

'It's a hoody, Dad. Everyone wears them. And hood up is the style.'

'It's true, Jackson. Even I know that.' Normally she'd have made him remove the hood in a flash, but suddenly Jack had an ally in his mother. So keen was she to object to everything that his father said that she was siding with Jack even when she didn't agree. 'You keep it on, Jack.'

This was going to be easier than he thought. But then . . . 'So why did you want to invite Prince William for tea?' she asked suddenly. 'You've never wanted to be friends with him before.'

Why indeed? Jack thought. So I can get him to face down an evil pig-god and turn the tide of death, actually, Mum. He wasn't sure how that would go down. Then he had a brainwave. He took a deep breath. 'I thought he might be able to give us some advice.'

'What on? Clothes?' scoffed Lord Bootle-Cadogan. 'Do you think he wears these . . . hoodlums?'

'Hoodies, Dad, and yes, I bet he does. I also bet he knows what to do about . . .' Did he dare say it? It was a bit of a wild card, but there was definitely a bit of the gambler in him, taking after Jay and Johnnie with the Ear Lobes as he did. '. . . about back pay for servants and all that. I mean, who has the most servants in the country? The royal family, I bet.'

Lord Jackson paused with his soup spoon halfway to his mouth, and from beneath the rim of his hood Jack saw his father's eyes narrow. He was hooked. 'Hmm. We'd need to talk to the Queen about that, surely. Or Charlie boy at the very least.'

'The Queen isn't going to come and visit us here, Jackson. Charles might, at a push, but I think Jack may have a point. William and Harry do seem very accessible.'

Wow. They were both hooked. 'True,' said his father darkly. 'Very true. Good lad, Jack. A prince. Well, we ruling classes should stick together. We'll make a lord of you yet.'

'Great,' said Jack in a small voice. That wasn't what he'd meant at all. Still, it was a means to an end . . . 'So you'll invite him? June twenty-first – three days away.'

'I'll talk to one or two of the boys at the club about how to get hold of him,' said his father, clearly quite intrigued now. 'Maybe the Old Etonians network. Did he go to Eton? I'll wager he did.'

Oh. That again. Jack drifted in and out during the rest of dinner, careful to say enough to keep his mother happy and prevent her from dashing round to feel his brow – his monobrow– and equally careful not to say too much of anything that might upset his father and divert him from his Prince William duties. The evening droned by, and it was with great relief that he was able to excuse himself and go to find Bone. Thankfully, his mother seemed to have forgotten to mention to Lord Bootle-Cadogan that their son was taking industrial action down at Bone's cottage.

Almost as if it had been planned, Bone cruised past

the graveyard on the way back and they leaped out for a couple of hours in the crypt – time for a game or two of Senet, and a Tahtib lesson from Albie. Then, happily exhausted, they returned to the cottage, where Bone nodded goodnight from his doorway and Jack fell into a bed that was so short his feet dangled over the end. It was the best night's sleep he'd ever had.

When he woke up, however, he felt slightly embarrassed at having made such a fuss about Bone not being a servant, as he had to ask him to do something very servanty straight off. 'Uh, Bone ... I've got basketball this morning ... I need a shave – if you don't mind.'

It wasn't going to disguise his too-long nose and pointy ears, but he hoped that as long as he wasn't covered in blue-black fur and he jumped around at the back for the whole game he might get away with it. Bone sighed, then jerked his head towards the living room where he kept the razor and mirror.

A few minutes later, Jack inspected Bone's handiwork in the little bronze disk. 'I look like some kind of mutant. Or one of those disgusting dogs that are all skin, like they've been turned inside out.' Beneath the fur, his skin was mottled and dark, and his jaw

129

and ears were definitely more canine than human. 'What'll I do? If I don't go to practice, I'm off the team.'

Bone studied him for a while, then held up a finger. He disappeared and came back with several rolls of the bandages he'd been wearing when he first arrived in Lowmount after his sojourn in Syria and Egypt, then proceeded to wrap up Jack's head until it resembled a wasps' nest. 'How's that going to help?' he yelped through the gap Bone had left in the crepe so he could breathe and eat his breakfast.

Bone held up another finger, then headed outside to the Daimler, revved the engine and drove it straight into a huge sycamore tree by the driveway, which Jack didn't remember being there yesterday. As Jack studied the tree, wondering if seeing fully grown trees that hadn't been there before was a particularly useless new dog-god power, Bone came back in looking rather smug and held out his arms like a magician who'd just pulled off a major stunt.

'Aha!' said Jack. 'We had a car accident, I bashed my face to bits, but look – I'm still here! Look how committed to basketball I am! Yeah. By the way, my father is going to kill you.'

Bone shrugged. Don't care, said his body language.

'Especially if Prince William comes to tea. I'll have to try to bend it all back into place after school,' said Jack. As he was largely god at the moment, he figured it should be possible. 'Or you could. You're pretty strong, Al-Bone.'

Bone scowled. Yep, thought Jack. Looked like he would have to do it himself.

Even with the shaving and bandaging, Jack managed to arrive at school a few minutes early. There were definite advantages to living in a small house instead of an enormous stately home – not having to run four miles because he'd left his bag in his bedroom, for instance, or being able to get down to breakfast in less than thirty seconds, and eat it in thirty more seconds as it was just cereal. Coco Pops. He didn't have those at the castle.

Several of the minutes he'd gained were then taken up explaining to Fraser and Minty and the rest of the team why his head was bandaged, and pointing out the ding in the front of the Daimler as Bone swept ostentatiously up and down the school drive. Fortunately the sight of the stoved-in radiator silenced even the most boisterous of his teammates, and Fraser made them go easy on him in case he had concussion.

He hung around in defence, marking Minty, recalling how terrified he'd been of her the first time he'd had to do that. She wasn't really making it any easier on him this time, it was true, but at least now he knew that her bark was worse than her bite. Bark. Bite. Mmmm. Sounded fun. Through the slit in his bandages, Jack watched the ball fly towards Minty. Defend, Jack, he told himself. Now that he was no longer afraid of her, it was a lot easier to follow her arm up into the air as her hand reached for the ball. Defend. Bark. Bite. No, ummmm . . . what was it he was doing?

It was too late. He was aiming for the ball, but before his brain had a chance to connect with the rest of him, his slavering jaws burst out through the bandages and a set of vicious teeth connected with Minty's outstretched arm. She let out a horrified howl and thrashed her arm around, with Jack still attached to it, and then suddenly she looped her other hand around and punched Jack in the bandages. It worked; instantly Jack opened his jaws to say indignantly, 'Ow – I'm supposed to have concussion, you know,' and his grip on her arm loosened enough for her to extract it from his mouth. The ball, meanwhile, had gone out of play.

'Oh, Minty, sorry, sorry, I don't know what came over me. I was going for the ball, honestly.'

The other players were staring at them, confused, as Fraser hurried over with Guisely in hot pursuit. No longer content with watching from the sidelines, Mr Guisely was bearing down on Jack as if he might take a swing at him too, shouting, 'He bit her! Red card, ref! He bit the girl.'

'Wrong game, sir,' said Fraser quickly, firmly but politely getting in between Guisely and Jack. 'Jack, on the bench. Minty, are you OK?'

To everyone's astonishment, including Jack's, Minty simply stared at Fraser as if he was mad. 'He didn't bite me, Frase. I don't know what Gui — Mr Guisely is on about.'

The teacher gazed at her in disbelief. 'Miss West, I saw it with my own eyes. These are sniper's eyes. The boy sank his teeth into your arm just below the elbow. It's a wonder it's still attached.'

With a shrug, Minty held out both arms. There was not a scratch on either of them. Guisely reached out

133

and rotated each one with his thumb and forefinger, hardly able to believe it.

Fraser frowned. 'So what was all the hollering about?'

'That was me,' said Jack quickly. 'Hurt my head.'

'You don't have to cover for me, Posh,' said Minty just as quickly. Jack stared. 'The truth is, Fraser, he had the ball, and I couldn't believe he'd actually beaten me, and I sort of . . . lost my temper. Smacked him on his sore head.'

'Is that true?' Fraser asked Jack.

It was so far from the truth, and so uncharacteristic of Minty, that Jack wondered for a moment whether Seth was responsible for this. Perhaps he'd possessed Minty and temporarily turned her into a nice person to lull them into a false sense of security. But she looked perfectly normal, her usual bolshie self, so Jack gave way. 'Sort of. I was going to get the ball, and Minty caught me on the head with her hand. I'm sure she didn't mean to.' Any more than he meant to chew her arm like a pork chop. Her reaction was purely instinct, as his had been.

Unfortunately, his was the wrong instinct.

'Bench for both of them?' said Guisely hopefully.

'Let's take five,' said Fraser. 'And then we'll start again.'

He'd had a reprieve. Minty stalked off ahead of him and pretended to get a drink from the water fountain, jerking her head at him as she bent to it. He trotted over obediently. 'You have got to learn to control it,' she hissed, furious. 'What if it hadn't been me? You could have grabbed anyone's arm, or their throat, and I wouldn't be able to cover for you then.'

Jack scratched beneath his tattered bandages, and his finger rasped against the stubble on his cheek. His fur was back. 'I don't know how to,' he said. 'It's getting worse now that Seth is back in town.'

'You have to concentrate,' said Minty. 'And then you can pick your moments.'

'Do you mean,' said Jack, not quite daring to believe what she'd said, 'that I can choose to be Doghead whenever I like? And turn it off if it's not the right time?'

Minty wiped water off her chin. 'You don't ever see me with Hathor on my head at the wrong moment, do you? That's my choice. You're a god like me, and you have power. You just have to learn to use it.'

Jack nodded slowly. What Minty said was true – she was only ever hawk-headed when they were out of sight of everyone else, whereas his Doghead appeared seemingly at random. 'How?' he asked under his breath.

'I don't know how you do it,' said Minty. 'For me, I carry the picture in my head of what state I'm in, and it doesn't change unless I do it deliberately.'

'Like me when I Zip!' shouted Jack excitedly.

His cry attracted a bit of attention, and Minty rolled her dark eyes. 'Whatever,' she said. She bent to get another drink and then recoiled abruptly. Where previously there had been pure drinking water, now there was thick red liquid oozing up in a slow sloppy arc.

'You'd better learn quickly,' she whispered. 'That's the first plague – water turning into blood.'

Jack nodded, trying to be as serious as he knew he should be when the 'tide of death' was upon them. He was so excited about the thought of being able to swap between states, though, that he could barely concentrate.

So that was how it was done. The picture – the mental image and the strange, unearthly pull and then the tighten-and-release of the Zip – that was how it was done.

He waited until all the other players had gone in, shouted, 'Loo break!' to Fraser, and Zipped into the toilets, figuring it was good practice.

First he checked a few of the taps. Water. For now.

Leaning on the sink, he focused all his effort on what he would look like as a boy again. Dark curly hair. Hooky nose. Tall with floppy ear lobes. There – the image was clear in his head. Whether it was fixed enough was another matter, but there was only one way to find out. Carefully he unwound the bandages and, to his great joy, a stubble-free, pink, human chin appeared in the mirror. He unwrapped more quickly. Red lips. Yes! A normal nose – still huge and beaky, but not an actual muzzle any more. Then his eyes, and then . . . hallelujah! Two eyebrows! He dragged the rest of the bandages off, Zipped twice around the playing field in a speedy victory lap, then raced into the gym to join the game.

All eyes turned to stare at him as he ran through the doors. Of course! They'd thought he had a bashed-in face – he ought to have at least pretended he had

137

a bruise or two. 'That's better,' he said quickly. 'I thought the bandages might be hampering my game. You can start again now.'

The team slowly formed a semicircle around him, and Fraser shook his head as if he wasn't sure what to say. 'Jack, is this a joke?'

'No, we really did smash the car up.'

'No, not that.' Fraser stared at his shoes. 'The costume.'

'Costume? I'm not in . . . oh.' 'Oh no' would be more like it. Pretending to scratch his head, Jack reached up a hand. As it glanced off his long, snuffly muzzle, he licked his own palm by mistake as his tongue was hanging so far out, and sure enough, when his hand got to the top of his head, his fingers met with pointy, furry ears.

Minty was staring at him with an expression of complete and utter disgust. Only Jack knew that she was ashamed of his being unable to control his powers effectively, other than for his bad sportsmanship in the field of basketball.

Which was why everyone else was disgusted at him.

'I . . . thought we might need a mascot,' he said,

trying to laugh in a 'jolly old me' sort of way but finding it came out as a strangulated little bark.

Fraser finally looked up from his shoe-studying. 'No, we don't need a mascot, Jack, we need a reliable player. Sorry, mate. You're out.'

It wasn't until he heard the words that Jack realized fully what being in the team meant to him. It was his only shot at being one of the gang. Normal. Accepted. And his stupid Doghead curse had blown it completely. Glad that dogs didn't shed tears, Jack slumped out of the room.

He decided on the way home. Enough was enough. He didn't want to be a god any more, or a dog, or anything in between. He just wanted to be normal. If he could spend a few days being normal, and being a major suck-up to Fraser, perhaps he would let him back on the team.

Of course he'd have to avoid all the others for a while. To make a start, he set off home on his own, running around and around the village under the glowering dark skies, but his bad mood, instead of going away, seemed to get worse and worse.

Why should he avoid the others? He was going to tell them. They'd all be waiting for him in the crypt; he could just go and make his announcement, and move out of Bone's, and go home and be an everyday future lord. There.

Sure enough, everyone was congregated around Granny Dazzle's tomb when he got there. Minty and

Hathor looked at him knowingly, and Jack suddenly realized that Hathor had been tracking him as he ran around Lowmount, trying to work off his fury.

That did it.

'You can all just stop trailing me, and don't bother looking so sorry for me either. I've made a decision. I'm just not doing it any more,' said Jack belligerently. 'I've had enough of being a freak, and now Minty's told me how I can be me all the time, I'm going to practise until I never turn into Anubis again. We've dealt with all the people in the graveyard anyway.'

'I never said you could do away with it altogether,' said Minty, feeding Hathor a dead mouse. 'You've been cursed. You can't just uncurse yourself.'

'It's true, Jack.' Albie was perched on top of the central sarcophagus, swinging his long legs as if enjoying the absence of arthritis. 'Anyway, from what you and Minty have said, it might take you a long time to master the art of avoidance.'

'I'll get there eventually.'

'It took me centuries to learn how to use my powers to the full,' said Minty dismissively. 'Even the basic stuff takes years. You do seem to be natural at some

141

stuff though – the Zipping and all that. Maybe it won't take you as long.'

'It won't.'

'But,' said Minty, 'what I did find was that everything takes a lot, lot longer if you're trying to do it just for yourself.'

'It's not just for me. It's for my . . . my family, and the basketball team.' Even Jack could hear how unconvincing he sounded, but he still didn't want to retract it. Let someone have a go at him if they wanted. He was ready.

Albie barked out a short laugh. 'Well, as long as the *basketball team* survives . . .'

'What about us, Jack?' said Ice, fixing him with her cool blue eyes.

'Yes, Jack, about us what?' added Ozzy.

There was a very unfamiliar feeling in the pit of Jack's stomach. He didn't like it, and he wanted to reject it, but somehow it was egging him on to say cruel things. 'Here's a thought,' he said suddenly. 'Maybe if I can control my dogheadedness, Ozzy'n'Ice'n'Ice'n'Ozzy, maybe you two can control your stupid repeating obsession. I mean, it's not as if "about us what" even makes sense, is it?'

Ozzy stared at him, bewildered. 'Is it not?'

'Don't even start, Ice,' said Jack quickly. 'Not is it. It not is. Snotty snot. It just won't work.'

Ice opened her mouth to say something and then shut it again quickly, and she and Ozzy shrank back simultaneously, their presence diminishing along with their size and the strength of their colours.

Jack felt a chill run down his neck, where the fur ended and the skin began. He looked up to find Granny Dazzle's ghostly outline glaring down at him; he could feel the disapproval even in the way she was hovering over him. Well, what could she do? She was only a ghost.

'That was rather cruel and unnecessary, Jack,' said Albie coldly. 'I don't really know why I'm surprised, of course, but I find that I am. You keep insisting that you are different from your family, and yet you're just the same.'

'What's that supposed to mean? Oh, don't tell me – all these "ruling classes" are cruel and unnecessary, is that it?'

'Something like that,' said Albie, and to Jack's shock he jumped down from the sarcophagus and squared up to him.

So that was how it was going to be. 'I can take you, Albie,' he said angrily. 'Especially without your special little fighting stick.'

'I'll risk it,' said Albie.

They glared at each other, Jack mystified as to how it had suddenly ended up that he was about to fight his best friend, horrified that the feeling in his gut made him want to smack Albie straight in the middle of his shiny, trusting face, and yet somehow unable to resist. His fist was rising of its own accord; he could already taste the satisfaction he was going to get from planting one on Albie, but he didn't want to feel it . . . shouldn't feel it . . .

'Fight it,' insisted a voice beside him.

'Don't want to,' he said.

Someone shook him by the shoulders. 'This isn't you, Jack,' said the voice again. 'You can control it as you can your appearance. Like I said, the things you do for others are easier to learn. Fight it, Jack.'

He knew the voice. He often found it very irritating, but now it was especially annoying, because he knew it was right. Fight it . . . Fight Albie. No! Not Albie. Albie was his friend. Fight the nastiness. He focused his attention on the nagging unpleasantness in his stomach, and suddenly he realized what it was. Seth. He was what was making Jack feel this way. And the voice was Minty, his friend and supporter, and the person he was about to thump was . . . his best friend. Albie.

'Albie,' he said suddenly, 'what . . . what am I doing?'

'You're threatening to thump me, old chap,' said Albie menacingly. 'Queensberry rules, I trust.'

Jack shook himself down. 'No, I wouldn't . . . I'm sorry. It's not me.'

Albie glared at him for a long moment. His eyes looked clear to Jack – not as if he was possessed at all, but simply angry with Jack for some unknown reason, so angry he was prepared to get into a scrap with him.

Jack backed away. 'I'm sorry. I need to . . .'

He felt sick to the core. How could either of them be acting this way? It had to be Seth – turning water to blood, threatening them with tides of death. What else would he be up to? Without stopping to plan it out, Jack Zipped to the computer in his mother's study. It wasn't until he was safely installed in her empty seat that he thought about how it had become second nature to Zip, to skulk about avoiding his parents, to investigate Egyptian plagues with barely a shudder. Maybe this was . . . his normality?

Shaking himself, Jack Googled 'plagues'. A list of pages about the 'ten plagues of Egypt' popped up on the screen. He read a few, learning that the plagues had been sent by God to punish the Pharoah for keeping the Israelites as slaves. The plagues were pretty gruesome – just the sort of thing that would appeal to an evil pig-face like Seth.

Water turning to blood to kill all the fish – that was the first one. Yuck. Suddenly he remembered the blood on the ceiling and the edges of the papyrus – it had dissolved into pure water, like the drinking fountain. So Seth was already visiting one plague upon them. They could apparently expect plagues of frogs, gnats, flies, diseases in livestock and boils on people, before the really exciting stuff like hail and fire and swarms of locusts were unleashed.

But it was the ninth and tenth plagues that really worried him. Number nine – darkness. He didn't even need to look out of the window to know that it was unnaturally dark outside. It had been for days. Seth's influence was already stretching into their world. And then the tenth plague, the most horrible of all – the death of the firstborn of every family. For some reason Jack pictured little Joseph, with Buttons, scuttling away from Seth the pig as the evil one roared with mocking laughter. He hadn't got him this time, but it was almost as if he was toying with his food. And all the rest could be just around the corner if they didn't deal with this.

Forget 'they'. It could all descend upon them if *Jack* didn't deal with this. All at once, Jack couldn't stand his own selfishness. Maybe Albie was right, and the Bootle-Cadogans couldn't help but be cruel. It didn't feel like him though. This bitter pulse running through him was not Jack's usual state of being. He was part Carruthers as well, and Granny Dazzle had never been anything but kind. That must be why her ghost had looked so testy in the crypt.

He couldn't give up. Furthermore, he didn't want to give up. He wanted to help.

In less than a minute he was back at the crypt. Albie stirred nervously at the sight of him, but Jack's anger had completely disappeared. He redirected his focus to his appearance, and to his relief he felt his hair, his teeth and his nose recede. 'Yes!' He could control it even when he was in his Doghead domain!

All at once his friend's expression changed, and Albie started to laugh. 'You've still got the ears, you nincompoop.'

'Oh. Yes, wait.' Jack closed his eyes and pictured long, dangly ear lobes, and when he opened his eyes again he could see from Albie's expression that he'd got it right this time. 'Well, that was all horrible,' he said cheerfully.

Albie sighed. 'It always was.'

Jack was just about to ask him what that meant when Ozzy emitted a short moan. He ran around the altar table. 'Ozzy'n'Ice, I'm so sorry. That was Seth and his darkness making me say that stuff. I think it's cute, your repeating thing. Cute it is,' he added for good measure.

'That is not why I moaned,' said Ozzy, although Jack noticed that Ice covered her mouth to stop herself echoing him. 'No. There is news from the transmitter of the waves.'

'Is it bad?'

'Bad it . . . yes,' said Ozzy. 'There is fear and anger again across the airwaves, and the man with the bad breath needs help.'

'The man with the bad breath?' Jack wondered what on earth he was on about. Did he mean his father? What would he be doing at the holiday park? Then suddenly he got it. 'Oh, you mean the man with the bad *breathing*.'

'Yes,' said Ozzy and Ice together. Ice went on, 'The pig is there again, and the bad-breathing man is breathing badly. Very badly.'

And just as Jack and Albie were staring at each other, the mobile in Albie's deep pocket chimed. Albie exclaimed in surprise, looking like he'd forgotten it existed.

'It's not my father, is it?' said Jack.

Albie shook his head, and withdrew another phone from his other pocket, which Jack recognized as the one his mother called Bone on. 'No, it . . . I've never had a call on this phone before. Someone's calling the undertaker.'

'Oh! I suppose that's you.' Jack had never really thought about it before, but since Wee Willie Waite had died (having had a heart attack at the sight of a mummy marauding through the village), it made sense that the only living relative and trained undertaker, Will's brother Albie Cornthwaite, was now in charge of the undertaking business. Though as nobody else ever saw Albie in his youthful state, or knew that he and Bone were one and the same person, it would make it impossible for him to claim the family cottage as his own or take over the business properly.

'It was the only thing I took after Will died,' said Albie sadly. 'In case anyone ever needed Waites' Undertakers again.'

The phone was still ringing. 'It sounds like someone does. You'd better answer it,' said Jack.

Albie lifted the phone to his ear and pressed the little green telephone symbol. Silence descended over the crypt.

'Albie, you're not Bone now, you have to speak,' said Jack. Grabbing the phone off his friend, he put on his most official voice. 'Waites' Undertakers – can I help you?'

'Oh, yes, thank goodness,' said a female voice, sounding a little teary. 'The most dreadful thing happened – Mr Catlow got all worried about the pig being at large again, and he got very agitated and then he . . . he died. Here at work! I'm his secretary. Do you think you could come and . . . take care . . . you know . . . of the . . . of him?'

'We certainly can,' said Jack. 'Where is that?'

'The Tall Trees Holiday Park.' The woman sniffed miserably as the location sprang up in Jack's mind. Aha – that place again. He cleared his head quickly in case he Zipped without planning to. She was still talking. 'Poor Mr Catlow. And now I've got to tell his wife!'

'All right, you get on with that,' said Jack gently. 'We'll be there in two minutes.'

'Two minutes? But you're fifteen miles away!'

'Figure of speech,' said Jack hastily. 'I meant – just as soon as we can.'

'Thank you,' said the woman. 'I'll leave him on the desk.'

She rang off, and Jack handed the phone back to Albie. 'That's all a bit weird,' he said. 'A man has died at the sinister holiday park and now his body's draped over a desk and his secretary wants us . . . well, you . . . to go and deal with it.'

'He wasn't mauled by a wild boar?'

'Not sure, but it sounds like he died of . . . anxiety.'

Albie scratched his head thoughtfully. 'Right, I'd better go and grab a coffin and some stuff.'

'Like a body bag?' said Jack, almost excited. 'It's a bit like a cop programme, isn't it?'

'I was thinking of embalming fluid,' said Albie. 'Perhaps you'd better bring some of your own professional bits and pieces with you too.' He nodded towards the portmanteau.

They set off moments later with the portmanteau stashed in the back of the Daimler. Once at the undertakers', they transferred it to the back of the hearse and slid an empty walnut coffin in beside it, filled with bottles and bandages that would help Albie in the mummification process. There was no doubt in either of their minds that a full mummification would be necessary. This body was in close proximity to Seth, and the dead man needed protection.

Maybe they all did. But this was somewhere to start.

15

'Go up to the main gates and speak into the intercom thing,' said Jack. 'Perhaps if we stay in the car those snakes won't be able to attack us.'

'Sir.' Bone switched on the windscreen wipers to knock off the few black asps that had already rained down on them, and they both tried not to listen as the wheels crunched over the heaving mass of snakes. Jack leaned across him as they reached the park. 'Undertaker,' he said crisply into the intercom, and the large barred security gate swung slowly open.

As soon as they were beyond the trees the sky seemed much clearer, and Jack could see that there were still a few holidaymakers at the park, although they didn't look terribly happy. Gone were the cosy days of smiley faces sausage-sizzling on a sunny deck. 'This won't be good for business, us driving through the place in a hearse.'

Bone raised an eyebrow. Maybe, maybe not, his expression said.

'Well, how could it be good for business? Oh! I suppose it might be good for your business.'

Bone simply nodded. It was true. Bone did have a business – or at least he should, if he could claim it as his own. This was the first newly dead person that Bone had had to work on, and Jack was quite intrigued to see how it all went, but if it went well, being an undertaker could be so much better than just being classed as a servant of the Bootle-Cadogan family.

They drove through the copse of trees that surrounded the central park facilities, including the wave pool and the management offices. Jack peered upward, expecting to see snakey black rods hailing down on them, but to his surprise they were deluged with the little propeller-shaped seed pods that spiralled down from the sycamore trees. Beneath the car lay a thick carpet of them. It still didn't feel right – more autumnal than summery – but it was better than smearing the windscreen with smashed-up snakes.

Finally they rounded a corner and cruised straight up to the service entrance of the enormous glass building at the centre of the holiday park. Jack stared at it. 'Bone, have you seen what it is?'

'Sir?'

'Stop the car a second,' said Jack, 'and look up.'

Awestruck, they both stepped out of their seats and stared up at the vast glass building before them. Four sloping sides made completely of huge panes of glass rose up in a peak, and the point at which they met was coated in what looked like . . . gold.

Bone's jaw dropped as he pointed at the golden pinnacle.

'That's a . . . a capstone, right?' said Jack. 'Which means that whole building is, um, a pyramid. A glass pyramid.' Jack nodded slowly, taking it all in. 'A pyramid. With a golden capstone. And a dead person inside it. Nice.'

Jack felt suddenly fearful, the hackles on the back of his neck bristling urgently. 'We'd better go in,' he said, not because he wanted to find the dead body but because he really, really wanted to get out of the way of the snake-spitting trees and any large pigs that might be running around.

'Sir!' coughed Bone, and he nodded towards Jack's dog-head.

'Oh. Yes, maybe I'd better try to change that.'

Tempting as it was to strut around as Anubis, Egyptian God, inside a ready-made pyramid, it didn't seem fair to the park guests or to the poor secretary who had called the undertaker. If people were dropping dead from fear of a wild animal, then the last thing they needed to see was a tall muscly boy with canine features.

Dropping down so that he could see himself in the wing mirror, Jack closed his eyes and pictured his normal Bootle-Cadogan features. This time he tried to breathe deeply throughout the process; he wasn't sure why, but he felt as though that might help.

Eventually Jack opened his eyes. His nose was back to normal. That was progress, at least. 'Come on. Let's go and find Mr Dead Person.'

By arguing with the security guard over the inter-com, they managed to get the service doors made of smoked glass to slide apart so they could drive the hearse straight into the belly of the building. The service road continued down a narrow corridor, and in the distance they could see the glint of water.

'That must be the wave pool,' said Jack. 'Let's not drive in there, Al-Bone,' he added sharply.

Bone was staring ahead dreamily, and to Jack's

horror his friend's eyes suddenly filled with tears. 'What?'

'Sir,' said Bone crossly, wiping his sleeve across his face and refusing to look at Jack. Back off, in other words.

Jack had annoyed his friend once too often of late – there seemed to be a new unpredictable level of unhappiness to Al-Bone's mood that was more than just Seth-induced depression – so he simply averted his eyes politely from Bone's tear-streaked face and jumped out of the car. Dragging the coffin and the portmanteau into the service lift, Jack hit the button marked 'Management Services' and watched Bone out of the corner of his eye. He was starting to get that stubborn set to his jaw that came about whenever they talked about Jack's father; the same look, in fact, that he'd had as Albie when he was about to start scrapping with Jack in the crypt. 'This is our floor!' he called too loudly, trying to lighten the atmosphere.

Bone relieved Jack of the portmanteau and they each dragged their item out into the corridor and left them on one side, then looked around for some indication of where to go. The place looked deserted, with several empty offices stretching away down one side of the corridor.

The other side of the corridor was a plate-glass window, through which the whole of the interior of the pyramid could be viewed. 'Handy for spotting people bombing in the wave pool,' said Jack, looking down on the scene with amazement. There was a whole tropical wonderland down there, with lap pools and waterfalls and spas dotted around between the palms, and lush ferns dipping their fronds into the edge of the enormous central wave pool which had a whole playground of slides and helter-skelters cascading from an island in its middle. It looked like a heap of fun.

Beside him, Bone gazed down on it too, shaking his head again, as though trying to recollect something. Then he breathed on the window and sketched out a word.

'Abydos,' read Jack. Whoever Abydos was, he or she was clearly playing on Bone's mind. Bone pointed down into the pools, and then underlined the misty word. 'Abydos – I don't know what that means. You'll have to . . .'

'Oh! You must be the undertaker,' called a voice

along the corridor. Bone leaned casually against the word on the glass and wiped it away with his shoulder as a kind-faced woman in her fifties trotted up the corridor towards them. When she got close enough to see them both properly, she stopped short, and Jack worried for a second that his dog-head had returned. But then she frowned. 'You're very young,' she said suspiciously. 'Are you sure you know what you're doing?'

'He does,' said Jack, pointing at Bone. 'His family has been in the undertaking business for hundreds of years. Maybe thousands,' he added helpfully. Both Bone and the woman stared at him. 'Anyway, I'm very confident we can deal with your situation here. Ignore me – I'm his apprentice – and here for the heavy lifting. Could we see the corpse?' Bone kicked him on the ankle. 'Sorry, I mean, the deceased?

The woman seemed reassured. 'Yes, of course. I'm so glad you could come so quickly. The police came immediately with the doctor, and they confirmed it was a heart attack, so Mr Catlow –' she paused to extract a handkerchief from her sleeve – 'Mr Catlow's body, I should say, has just been lying here. Looking at me. It's been awful.'

Bone patted her on the back as they followed her towards a door labelled 'Boardroom', and Jack called out, 'Don't worry, Mrs . . .'

'Sombourne,' she sniffed.

'Mrs Sombourne. We'll take over from here.'

Mrs Sombourne sighed. 'Oh, thank you. It's been such a day. You see, when the pig started running around the park again, Gordon – Mr Catlow – said that everyone should go back to the chalets and stay inside, and I made him coffee and then I went off for lunch. And when I came back . . .' She drew a trembling hand to her mouth. 'Oh, it was so awful. He'd been drinking coffee all morning, even though we both knew he really shouldn't, and pacing around trying to get everything sorted out, and he came out in a nervous rash, which made him even more agitated . . . And his heart was very weak so he shouldn't have had all that stress and coffee, the doctor said, but how was I to know that?' At that, Mrs Sombourne's chest started to heave dangerously.

Recognizing the onset of a crying fit from a lifetime spent in the same house as his mother, Jack held up a hand. 'That's fine! You couldn't have known that, of course. You go and make yourself a nice cup of, well, tea, and we'll sort out Mr Catlow.'

'No more questions?' quavered Mrs Sombourne, brushing down her pink cardigan. 'I really couldn't bear it.'

'Not a word,' said Jack. He waited until she was out of the room, then hurried over to join Bone. 'This is all a bit weird, isn't it?'

Mr Catlow was stretched out on the board table, his chubby form spreading towards the edges in a fleshy puddle. Bone was studying him carefully, and finally rolled out his wallet of utensils and extracted a hook.

'Don't you need to take out his organs first?' He'd watched Bone embalm Will Waite's body in the past, so knew the process involved putting organs in jars, stuffing the body with natron and basting it in embalming oil.

Bone grimaced and pointed to his watch. No time. He was going to hook out his brain, but leave the other organs for now.

But Jack still had his own role to play as Anubis. 'What about weighing his heart though? If Seth's running around out there, I'd like to pass Mr C.'s soul through to the Field of Rushes quickly.'

Bone nodded to him respectfully.

'Not too bad for your apprentice?' Jack laughed. 'I'll go and get the scales and the Feather of Ma'at from the suitcase,' he said, turning away quickly as Bone began to poke his long hook up the dead man's nose.

It was weird how life turned out sometimes. And death, thought Jack as he headed back down the corridor to retrieve the rest of the tools. As he rounded the corner in the corridor, a flash of pink shot into the lift and Jack froze. It looked very much as though Mrs Sombourne had been snooping around the portmanteau. Just as he turned to tell Bone, he heard the breath catch in his friend's throat.

Where the hook had dislodged the collar of Mr Catlow's shirt, they could both see the 'nervous rash' that Mrs Sombourne had talked about. It was like no rash that Jack had ever seen: great pustulous lumps rippled under the raw skin like something alive, and when Bone cautiously extended the hook and pulled off a couple of the man's shirt buttons, they could see that the lumps covered his entire torso, like hideous acne.

'Are those . . . boils?' said Jack.

He hardly had to wait for Bone's nod to know that he was right. Mrs Sombourne had a funny idea of a 'rash'. In fact, she seemed to have a few funny ideas altogether . . .

Jack was just next to her office, so he reached out and shook the handle softly. Locked. Of course. But that was no obstacle to Jack, and secretaries in fluffy cardigans weren't the only ones who could snoop. Picturing the inside of the office, Jack faded through the wall.

It looked normal enough – filing cabinets, desk and in tray, coffee machine, all arranged around the connecting door to Mr Catlow's office. But when he looked again, Jack noticed that the coffee machine was flooding the top of the cupboard on which it sat, spewing out coffee at double speed, so much so that it was spilling over into the fish tank beside it – a fish tank that seemed to be home to a dozen warty frogs who were casually snapping up food from a swarm of flies and mosquitoes that clouded the top of the tank. What had she said? They both knew he shouldn't have so much coffee. So why was she making so much? And why did she keep frogs in the office?

Jack sprinted around to the other side of the neat

desk and pulled open the drawer. On top of a pile of stationery was a file, and he read the name on it with a sinking heart: 'Gordon Catlow. Hired 10 June'. He'd only been there a few days, poor guy. Opening the file, Jack pulled out the top piece of paper. It was the results of Mr Catlow's medical.

'"Mr Catlow has a congenital heart problem, which is made worse by his excess weight and refusal to look after himself. He should be avoiding all stress and stimulants. You should not hire him under any conditions. Doctor Andrew Corrigan." Blimey!' said Jack.

His own heart plunged into his stomach. Something was becoming very clear. Mr Catlow had been set up. The heart attack had been induced.

But why would someone do that? Who would want to murder Mr Catlow? Jack paused for a second, then went to the computer and carefully keyed in a word. SOMBOURNE.

When he read what Sombourne meant, his heart sank still further. That was why someone had wanted to kill the man. Mr Catlow was just the bait. He and Bone were the ones who had been set up.

He pictured Bone poring over Mr Catlow's body

and Zipped there in a nanosecond. 'Al-Bone, we've got to get out. It's a trap. Mr Catlow was sick and someone killed him deliberately, and Sombourne is old-fashioned English for "piggery", so . . . a pig-person killed this man, knowing that you'd come and deal with the body and I'd come with you.'

Bone was staring over his shoulder, down through the windows overlooking the wave pool, his eyes misty with memories and something else – fear. Jack followed his gaze and felt sick. The edges of the wave pool were turning red.

'We're trapped,' squeaked Jack. 'And from here we can't protect Ozzy.'

'How true,' said a sweet female voice in the door-way.

And as they both turned in horror, the pink cardigan of Mrs Sombourne turned green and her powdery face exploded before their eyes until a swirling pig-head, complete with watery snout, filled the doorway. Then it disappeared as the door slammed and locked, and Jack heard the portmanteau contents shatter as a green vortex blew it apart.

16

Jack gazed in horror at Bone, and as his concentration slipped he felt his head morph back into its canine version, the jaw extending and dripping with saliva; coarse hairs springing through his pores and covering his face with a shadow, then stubble, then fur; ears shifting around his head and rustling with bristles. As they formed properly his hearing sharpened, and across the whole of the park he could make out the terrified screams of the holidaymakers, and one small voice which was almost paralysed with fear, but could still whimper, 'Buttons! Buttons, it's the bad pig. Talk now, Buttons. Buttons!'

'He's got the little boy; Seth's got Joseph,' Jack whispered to Bone, already preparing to leap out of a window.

'Sir, sir!' Bone grabbed him by the back of his shirt and tried in vain to pull him back.

Jack fought him off feverishly. 'I know he's luring

me out into the open, but I don't care. I promised that boy that Buttons would speak to him again if something really bad happened. I have to help him.'

'Ngggg!' Bone was running round and round the boardroom table, gathering hooks and canopic jars and stuffing them into his pockets. He gesticulated wildly at the scarlet frill of blood around the wave pool, looking as though he would drag Jack out by himself if he had to.

'I know, the tide of death.' Jack shrugged helplessly. 'But I have to keep my promise. And anyway, maybe this is the tide – water turning to blood, frogs and flies and boils, the darkness – maybe the death of firstborn children is next.'

'Sir, nooo! Nnngggh!'

Bone appeared to have lost his mind. He had Jack by the collar and was almost shoving him through the window in his desperation, and there was a wild look in his violet eyes that Jack couldn't quite place. Perhaps he needed to run from Bone too . . . 'Go and get the hearse,' he said firmly. 'You'll be safe. I'll check on the boy, but that's all, and then you can meet me at the main gate and we'll get the heck out of here.'

'Nngggh, nngggh, ssssir . . .' groaned Bone,

grabbing at his hair so it stood up in unfamiliar scrappy tufts.

What Bone wanted to do – or to avoid – didn't become clear, however, because right at that moment an incredible gust of wind blasted straight across the park, rattling the pyramid in its steel foundations, and lifting the golden capstone from its position so that a ghostly echo whistled around the entire building: 'Anubis . . .' The air turned green around them and then froze on their lips, and it took a second or two for Jack to work out that it was a zesty, lime green, and the ice was clean and refreshing.

'Ozzy'n'Ice!' he screamed. 'Keep out of the park! Keep ooouuut!' His last word became a howl and he sent it heavenwards, back through the raised capstone and up into the skies. He had no idea whether they could hear him, but if their words could be carried to him on a wintry breeze, then maybe his own tortured howl could get to them too.

Bone stared at him, aghast, his eyes still wild and unfocused.

'Go,' said Jack. 'Get the car. Gate. Go!'

They were quite high up – four or five floors, by his estimation. Even though he'd never Zipped from a great height to a low one, Jack knew that it was his only chance to get out quickly, avoiding whatever might be still lurking in the corridor if Bone hadn't managed to shake it off. Holding his breath for a moment, he pictured Joseph's bunk bed – the top bed, where he'd been sitting. No! That would terrify him. The bottom one, where Jack had hidden . . .

While he was still in two minds the Zip process began. *Vumphhhh!* He shot through the window and out into the open air. He found himself hovering face down like a freefall parachutist, twenty or thirty metres above the ground. Before he had time to scream, the ground was racing towards him, and in less than two seconds it was close enough for Jack to pick out individual bushes and the startled face of the security guard as he blasted past the first-floor window. If he'd really been a parachutist, it would have been too late, he realized – right about now he'd have been making a large X shape in the ground, with a dent where his canine nose sank in.

As it was, he hit the ground without feeling the impact at all. It was rather as if he'd landed face first in cotton wool, or on a large inflatable mattress like a stuntman. When he lifted his head, he found it was just above ground level. The rest of him was swivelling upright through the soil, upending geraniums and fuchsia faster than any mole. And then he was off, Zipping half in and half out of the ground, his shoulders and head appearing to slide along the turf ... the path ... soil ... tree roots ... the path again as he took the most immediate route across the holiday park to the chalet of the little boy.

Luckily the nearest way into the chalet from the wave pool was through a side wall and the family bathroom, then a quick shimmy across the hallway before he Zipped through the wall of the boy's bedroom and slid across on to the bunk.

It was only then that Jack appreciated just what havoc he had created by losing focus while he thought about where he was headed. Minty was right – he really needed to learn to concentrate. He hadn't been sure whether to aim for the top bunk or the bottom, and his godly powers had obliged by delivering him to both. His body from the chest down was housed in the lower bunk, while his shoulders and head stuck up through the mattress of the top one, so he looked like a head on a plate. A dog-head on a plate. What was worse was the fact that he'd been right in supposing the boy might be there. As Jack's head swivelled around the top bunk, he came nose to nose with Buttons, and the boy screamed at a million decibels.

Jack dragged his hands up through the mattress and clamped them over his ears. 'Ow! Don't do that . . . I . . . Buttons sent me a message to come and talk to you!' he hollered over the noise.

Joseph stopped yelling instantly, as if someone had flicked the off switch. 'Buttons? Did he?'

Phew, thought Jack. 'Yes, he said you were frightened and he wanted me to come and check on you.'

'But you're a big, scary dog-head thing.'

Jack tried to smile, then quickly stopped as the boy's face fell. With his dog-head grin, it probably looked like he was about to rip off the boy's arm. 'No, I'm sort of a teddy bear. Now, you just tell me what was scaring you.'

The boy's bottom lip quivered. 'It was the scary pig,' he whispered.

'Why are you whispering?'

'Because,' hissed the boy even more quietly, 'it's in my wardrobe.'

So it had been a trap, as they suspected! As the full enormity of what he'd just done sank in, Jack

Zipped himself free of the bunk beds. At the same moment the wardrobe doors flew open and vile-smelling green gas poured into the room.

Joseph was so terrified he was barely able even to scream as the swirling gases formed a whirlpool in which the face of a pig was quickly becoming discernible. Jack checked him over quickly. The boy was whiter than white; if he got any more scared he'd be joining Mr Catlow in the boardroom morgue.

He had to get him out of there. 'Where are your parents?'

'D-Daddy's gone to get the car, and Mummy's packing our suitcase.'

'Perfect,' said Jack.

Actually he wasn't sure if it was anything like perfect, as he'd never before tried what he was going to attempt now, but at least it meant that they were already planning to leave. Now they'd just be doing it more quickly.

The snout of the pig was forming, vicious tusks protruding beneath it. There was no time to spare. 'Grab Buttons,' said Jack to Joseph, picking the boy up under the armpits, 'and hold on.'

He vaguely remembered what the boy's mother

looked like. With the lad held firmly in his grip, Jack visualized her packing a case, and suddenly they were off, Zipping at the speed of light back through the bunk beds, straight through the wall and into the master bedroom on the other side. Sure enough, there was the mother folding clothes hurriedly into a suitcase laid out on the double bed. She looked up and let out an almighty scream.

'No time,' said Jack. 'But I'm here to help, seriously. What kind of car have you got?'

'Wh-what?'

'We've got a silver Mercedes C-class,' yelled the boy in Jack's ear.

'Impressive,' said Jack. 'Good boy.'

Before anyone else had time to scream, Jack said, 'Really sorry,' knocked the mother off her feet so that she sprawled on top of the suitcase, plonked Joseph down next to her, then pictured the car park on the far side of those horrible trees, honing down the image until he could feel that he was focusing on the right car. The instant the silver car appeared in his mind's eye he felt his limbs tightening. 'Hang on!' he called, and he grabbed both corners of the bed with all of his considerable might.

There was an instant in which the whole picture shimmied in his head. He wasn't going to be able to do it. Maybe it was because his feet were still on the floor. He was just about to jump on to the bed with the others when there was an almighty rending sound; to everyone's astonishment including his own, the walls ripped away from the building, the whole structure lifted slightly from the foundations and then they were off. The entire room, complete with three walls, a wardrobe and chest of drawers, and a double bed with three people, a suitcase and a stuffed rabbit on it, set off across the forest, melding itself around benches, parked bikes, trees, raining snakes, more trees . . . a fence . . . a Volkswagen camper van . . . all accompanied by the frantic screaming of the mother and the rumble of disintegrating plasterwork.

They slid to a halt around the silver Mercedes, so that it looked as though it had been parked on a stage set beside the bed. Joseph's father stared at them, bewildered.

'Cool,' murmured the boy.

'In the car, and get out of here,' said Jack quickly. He slammed the suitcase shut and threw it into the boot, ignoring the million questions that formed on

174

the man's face. 'I'll make sure you get a full refund,' he added, before picturing the wardrobe again.

Zummmph! He was off again, ploughing back through the trees. This was definitely the way to get through them, he decided – only partly there, sliding along at the speed of light, so fast that the snakes which poured like sump oil out of the tree trunks barely touched him . . .

And then one managed to coil itself around Jack's ankle. 'No!' he screamed, more angry than scared. How could that have happened? He was travelling at godly warp speed, so fast that molecules didn't even have time to form themselves properly into objects, and yet this stupid black cobra had somehow got hold of him. A stab of fear sliced through him. These were not normal snakes, of course. He couldn't afford to underestimate his enemy. Seth was going to bring Jack down, right there in the forest.

And the scenario only got worse as Jack heard the stately progression of the hearse through the park. 'Put your foot down, Bone,' he screamed, putting one of his own down on the head of the cobra. It splattered like a balloon filled with water, inky drops spraying out in a wide arc across the forest floor. Jack watched in horror as each droplet that touched the floor became a sickening black worm which then stretched and grew into an asp, some even widening at the head as they swelled before his eyes – more cobras.

Far from driving faster, Bone had stopped the car. He'd jumped out and was trying to run towards Jack, striking at the attacking snakes with his fighting stick, whimpering as they clutched at his legs, his wrists, coiling around his knees and wrapping themselves around the stick so that it was weighted down and he could no longer swing it.

'Bone, go back!' cried Jack. Snakes were writhing around him up to his knees, and were reappearing as fast as he could bat them aside. He could feel their fangs glancing harmlessly off his legs – at least, he assumed it was harmlessly. Who knew how much venom was being pumped into his veins, being stored up for when he became just a boy again and it could fell him instantly, or whether they'd find some soft bit of skin behind his knee that was vulnerable to attack, where a juicy cobra could sink its teeth in up to its gums and tumble him effortlessly.

And Bone . . . Bone wasn't a god, couldn't fight them off like Jack could. Yes, he was strong, and had lived a long time, but with the mass of snakes settling around them, Bone's terror was written all over his face. It was only a matter of time before they'd be completely overwhelmed, and before anyone realized where they might be, they could be completely swamped. They'd turn into peat, be discovered like bog men – well, he'd be a bog boy – buried in the ashes of snakes . . . too many snakes . . .

That was it! 'We have to go to the source,' shouted Jack.

'Sir?' croaked Bone, trying in vain to thwack an approaching black mamba with the wad of snakes that were coiled around his fighting stick. It was like hitting out with a large cotton bud.

'Don't bother attacking the snakes. Go for the trees!'

It was a good plan, in theory. Knock over the trees, or, better yet, rip them out at the roots, and the reptiles wouldn't be able to reproduce themselves.

There was a slight flaw in the strategy though – they couldn't move. They were both being swallowed up by the black mass, so many snakes that they seemed now to be one suffocating entity. Jack was forced backwards, staring up beyond the spewing treetops to

177

the sombre, swirling skies. There was a patch of army green above it, and his heart leaped.

'Ozzy'n'Ice! Help!'

Ice's anxious face appeared over the edge of the camp bed from the museum, magicked aloft by their special powers. 'Ozzy is gone,' she cried. 'Alone I am weak.'

Jack's heart plunged again. That was so much bad news all wrapped up in one. Ozzy gone – which meant they'd failed in their mission to protect him. Which meant Seth would be more able to get on with whatever he was doing to bring about the tide of death. Furthermore, Ice alone couldn't help them, so Bone and he were going to be smothered by snakes at any moment.

'Ice, can you attack the treetops?'

'I will try!' came the faint reply.

A bitter wind ripped through the forest, and to Jack's delight the tops of the trees directly under Ice turned glistening white, grew brittle and then snapped off as the chilled tornado tore at them. Icicles plunged to the floor like daggers, slicing through snakes as easily as if they were sushi. An especially large one whistled past Bone, almost decapitating him.

'Ice, careful!' screamed Jack as Bone's spectacles froze over his shocked eyes.

'Too much it is!'

'Get help.' Jack didn't even have the strength to shout any more, as the snakes tightened around his throat.

'My sisters!' called Ice, way above their heads. The sound echoed around the park like the cry of a dying swan. 'My sisters, come to me! Help us.'

The ground trembled. Jack wondered if it was an earthquake. No, there it was again, a distinct tremor through the earth's crust. Ice's sisters must be *big*, he thought. Unless of course it was just more bad luck and they were about to tumble into a boiling, lava-filled crevasse and not stop until they hit the earth's core. *Zzii*—

It was his final thought as a python curled itself around his head, covering his eyes, and he had one lucid moment to remind himself to clear his mind of the mental picture of the earth's superheated core. He noticed it was raining. Raining silver. Not asps, this time, but silvery little helicopters. Nice. He liked helicopters.

The next thing he knew, a tree root had sneaked

between the snakes and curled itself around his waist. It pulled, and he moved, up and across, out of the hideous mire of serpents and into the cloud of tiny silver rotary blades. Through the glittering, shifting curtain, Jack could see Bone appearing out of the blackness too, a slender arm of tree root pulling beneath his armpits. Jack followed the root. Where was that coming from? There was a whole network of them, swiping away snakes, penetrating the forest of evil pines and yanking them out with ease, choking the black floor with criss-crossing silver that squashed and flattened until the snakes were ground to dust.

Finally the air cleared, and Jack, who had thought that nothing much could surprise him any longer, nearly fainted at the sight of his rescuer. 'You're a sycamore tree,' he said in surprise.

'I am a tree goddess,' said the beautiful face above him. The face was the size of a VW camper van and sat atop a silvery, swan-like neck and shoulders that protruded from the foliage of the tree, which now looked like a rather spectacular ball gown. Jack swivelled; beneath the hem of the dress, the tree roots were drawing back, forming long, sinewy feet that looked capable of immense grace and dancing till dawn, as well as stamping out snakes and ripping up other trees. 'My sister Isis called for us.'

Jack was on a level with the face now. It was so vibrant and glowing that he was hardly able to look at it. 'Well, thank goodness she did,' he said. 'Where did you come from?'

'From far around,' said the tree goddess, pointing out the host of her sisters that stretched now across the forest. One was placing Bone back down near the hearse, and he was blushing like an idiot as he tried to stammer out a thank-you. 'We have been gathering around you all since the evil began. Have you not seen us, Anubis?'

Sycamores, thought Jack. 'Oh! Yes, I have – near the main building here, and around Lowmount, near Bone's cottage! Oh, and somewhere . . . somewhere else . . . That's it!' he shouted as a memory of Fraser and Bailey sheltering under a tree came back to him. 'By the gate of Clearwell Comp. I thought I'd never seen it before.'

The goddess smiled, half blinding Jack as she placed him back on the forest floor. 'That is correct. Now we return to our positions, for when we are next needed.'

'But . . . haven't you sorted it out now?' he said, confused. 'The snakes have disappeared. The trees are gone. And . . . oh no.'

Ice appeared next to him, on the flying camp bed. It looked oddly unbalanced – probably because he'd never before seen it fly without both Ozzy and Ice on board. 'Seth got him, didn't he?'

Ice nodded sadly. 'Get him he did. I know not where he is.'

'We'll find him, Ice, I promise,' said Jack.

But he had no idea how. And it felt like his promises were getting emptier by the minute.

17

The barque nudged the plinth on which the statue loomed, stretching well over a hundred feet above him. It had to be close to the size of Bartholdi's magnificent Statue of Liberty in New York, which Albie had never had the privilege to see but had read about with fervent obsession.

Albie craned his head back as the fringe of vines around the base of the coffin reappeared in order to drag them up the green onyx steps towards the statue itself. The statue was completely magnificent, and for the first time the enormity of what he had found hit him. Nobody had seen this before, nobody in living memory, at any rate. It was his own personal discovery. One day in the not too distant future, strangers would be reading about Albert Cornthwaite and how he was the first to lay eyes on the Abydos statue. It was an eighth Wonder of the World, rivalling the pyramids in the near vicinity, the lost Hanging Gardens of Babylon . . . He would be world famous. Rich. Independent. And very, very satisfied with his lot in life.

With an archaeologist's delicate touch, Albie let his hand trail from the coffin top along the green onyx steps. They were surprisingly warm, and looking up at the statue he found himself gently spattered with spray from the fountain, the silver-green light dappled through around the massive flail, Osiris's ear, his great green shoulder. For an instant Albie was transported back to Lowmount, to the trees in the copse beyond their undertakers' cottage, where he liked to lie and stare at the sky as he planned his escape from the village. The feeling was exactly the same: anticipation, great joy, and a sense of being at one with nature. 'Thank you,' said Albie respectfully. He wasn't quite sure whom he was saying it to – the bones in the coffin or the statue gleaming above him – but he was suddenly quite sure that Osiris had been with him all his life. He'd brought Albie here. This was Albie's destiny.

And finally they had reached the great green toe of the Osiris statue. It was just the little toe, and it was still as big as the coffin. They rounded several curves in the rock – more toes – until finally the coffin came to rest between the feet of the statue. As it settled on to the onyx-and-marble flooring like a dog before its master, Albie felt the vines that had held him in place begin to withdraw, until he was free to move independently. Of course. He had to get off or the coffin lid couldn't be opened.

'Terribly sorry,' he said, wondering if anyone could hear him. This didn't seem to be a place of ordinary senses like sight and sound, but rather of some primeval recognition that resonated somewhere in the soul, common communication needing no words. As if in response to this thought, the coffin quivered beside him, and the name 'ADJO' began to gleam with such brightness that Albie had to shield his eyes.

A beam of light shot up and out from each letter to meet the four jets of water so it was impossible to see where light ended and sparkling water began. As soon as all four had connected into great shafts of glistening ice, the vines spurted forth from the coffin, knocking Albie off his feet as they swept along the marbled floor and then extended in lacy green walls up the sides of the cavern, this time meeting up with the cascades of water from the central fountain. The effect was astonishing: suddenly the whole gigantic statue was encased in an egg-shaped lattice of silver filigree, which might have been water or light or some substance never before seen by man. Within the ovoid, four vertical curved bars of light-water embraced the statue like ropes, or like . . . like something Albie had seen but couldn't quite bring to mind.

The thunder of the shimmering curtain of water all around him was deafening. It was like standing inside Victoria Falls. Oddly, he was completely dry, and felt surprisingly unafraid . . . until the four bars of light linked directly with the corners of the coffin, sweeping him on to its lid again, and his head filled with the image that had been eluding him. That was what the four bars had reminded him of: a lift shaft. They were like the ropes at the corner of a lift capsule. Which could only mean that these beams of light-water had a job to do . . .

'Oh, good God above,' said Albie as he closed his eyes and felt the coffin lurch up into the air. Whether he meant his own God, or the god Osiris, he wasn't quite sure. He'd take whichever one would listen to him, frankly, because being hauled up the front of a hundred-odd-foot statue on a coffin hung from a shaft of light was beyond terrifying.

By the time he dared to open his eyes he was being transported past the statue's plaited beard. Then the mouth. Was the statue going to eat him? Albie squeaked. He could swear that he saw the marble lips curl upward at the corner, smiling in greeting. But no, now he was cruising on upward past the nose, the eyebrows, the smooth green forehead, and the direction he was taking became evident. They – Albie and the coffin – were being transported to the source of the enormous whale-spout of water ejecting straight from a hole in the crown of the statue's head.

They were going in.

Albie knew he should have been afraid, but some-how he felt an overwhelming calm. Nothing would harm him as long as he was treating the great Osiris with respect. It was obviously what he had been meant to do all along, after all. So he was about to drop through an aperture in the head of an enormous god-statue, riding an ancient coffin like a Roman chariot. So what? It was the most free, the most wonderful . . . the most alive that he had ever felt.

187

But then his human hearing picked out a voice, and the delightful sensations of readiness and acceptance fell away as if he was peeling off armour. Struggling to turn round, he followed the source of the noise – shouting and urgent screams.

'Master Cornthwaite, no! No!'

The boy was standing in the mouth of the tunnel, staring in horror at the vision of Albie about to be swallowed up into the head of a great statue.

Albie cupped his hands to his face. 'Adjo,' he screamed, 'go back! Tell Lord Bootle-Cadogan what you saw. But don't worry – it's fine. I'm fine!'

Adjo shook his head as if he couldn't hear. 'I heard you call my name, Master Cornthwaite. I came to save you. I will save you!'

And then, to Albie's horror, the boy flung himself across the open water towards the first stepping stone. He slipped, stumbled and slid beneath the surface.

Albie screamed from the depths of his lungs. 'Adjo, no! I didn't call! It was just the sarcophagus!'

His mind seemed to have stopped working. He couldn't go now, he just couldn't. He was on the brink of the biggest discovery of the modern age, of all time even. And he had been chosen for it – he, Albert Cornthwaite. Who knew what might happen if he halted the process for however long it might take to get to Adjo. It was just one boy. One small, insignificant Egyptian boy. He had to let him go. Didn't he? To find Osiris . . . the treasure of all their dreams . . . he had to let Adjo go . . .

He'd almost convinced himself that he could do it when the stricken face of the boy bobbed up above the surface, searching for him, and with a sickening lurch of his innards Albie realized what the expression on Adjo's face meant. He was still coming to rescue Albie. He had no thought for himself, only for his friend. And here was Albie considering . . . considering what?

'Stop!' Albie beat the coffin with his bare hands. 'Please stop – my friend is drowning!'

And in the very same moment that he spoke, the whole unified movement of light and water, coffin and statue, ground abruptly to a halt. Albie breathed out. He was going to be allowed to rescue the boy.

But then a crack appeared beneath his feet, the fissures shooting across the head of Osiris, splitting the marbled surface into a million green chunks that rained down upon the shoulders, which crumbled and fell away. As the statue disintegrated, Albie and the coffin plummeted down towards the water, and Albie's whole world turned deathly green.

18

They regrouped in the crypt, calling Minty on the way, and Jack related what had happened at the Tall Trees Holiday Park to his great-grandparents, Johnnie with the Ear Lobes and Minty, with Hathor cocking his head in beady-eyed interest. Ice perched herself on one end of the altar table, as usual, and then shifted along uncomfortably into the middle to fill up the empty space.

'I'll send Hathor to find Ozzy,' said Minty as soon as she'd heard what had happened. 'He'll have more chance of blending in than any of the rest of us.'

'Thanks,' said Jack. 'We still have to find the missing bit of his head too – or work out what to do with that perfume.'

He looked hopefully at his dead relatives, who were becoming ever more ghostly, so that Jack could only make out a pair of disembodied ear lobes, Granny Dazzle's feet and a floating handlebar moustache. The ear lobes and the moustache dipped down and up. Yes.

'We have to be quick too. The tide of death might have begun.'

Everything Jack held dear was under threat now. Mass destruction. No escape. And Jack could only begin to imagine the enormity of what Seth had in store. Which reminded him of what he and Albie had been busy doing at the holiday park.

'Oh! Is Mr Catlow in the hearse? Maybe we could pass him over. If he appears in ghost form he might be able to tell us something.'

Albie nodded. 'I pulled him down the corridor as soon as that secretary disappeared.'

'She turned into Seth and hid in a wardrobe, I expect,' said Jack.

'She'd had a good rummage through the portmanteau. Smashed everything.' Leaning over, Albie fished around under the altar. 'Fortunately this anointing liquid your forebears are so interested in was safely hidden under here.'

He pulled it out from its hiding place, and they all stared at it again. How on earth was a millilitre of golden liquid going to help? Especially if they had no

Ozzy to apply it to . . .

'We're running out of options.' Jack paused to remember the poem. 'Seth has Ozzy, and his uncrowned head, and besides, we don't know what we're meant to do with this stuff. And we certainly do not have a son of royal birth – even if we did we'd have to get him to the Tall Trees pyramid, somehow, to stop whatever Seth is up to.'

It was time to check in with his parents again. With any luck, Lord Bootle-Cadogan would have sent a florid invitation to Prince William that he couldn't possibly turn down. Quite how they were going to persuade him to go over to the holiday park and have a friendly chat with a green pig-headed monster Jack wasn't sure, but he'd cross that bridge when he came to it. It was nearly dinner time anyway, and Jack had devised a cunning plan to help him stay put in his boy features for the duration of the meal at least.

'Albie, I hate having to do this, and I know you don't normally have to turn up at dinner, but I need to look normal for a few hours. Could you hang around the dinner table and flash a photo of me as a boy at me if you see me slipping back into my doggy face?'

Albie sucked his teeth slowly, and Jack quailed. His friend looked furious, and yet he obviously felt as though he couldn't turn Jack down, no matter how much he wanted to. Then Jack remembered the curse on Albie's family too: to serve the Bootle-Cadogans as they served Seth. He'd managed to weaken the curse, but maybe it wasn't destroyed altogether. 'It's all right, you don't have to,' he said quickly. He'd find another way to deal with it.

'It's fine,' said Albie, although his face told Jack otherwise. 'Maybe you can throw me some scraps to eat afterwards.'

Ouch. Better try to joke about it, Jack decided. 'Hey, I'm the dog, remember? I'll have the scraps, thanks. You can put them in the bowl next to Roger's.'

'I might just do that.' Albie still looked a bit sniffy about it, but at least he had the grace to give Jack a small smile. 'So would you rather . . . eat next to Roger or your father?'

'Roger!' they said together.

It seemed to improve the mood. While Albie transformed into Bone the Butler, and Hathor the Hawk took off on his reconnaissance mission, Jack pocketed the vial of perfume and accompanied Ice down the tunnel to the museum. 'The best place to hide is probably inside one of the cabinets,' he told her, using the tiny key to unlock the display of Egyptian artefacts. 'Nobody will spot a garden gnome at the back.'

He waited until she'd shrunk to manageable size, and stowed her behind a canopic jar containing someone's gizzard, and a jagged chunk of wood that looked like driftwood, with part of the name of the ship carved into it: 'ADJC'. Ice blended in perfectly, and Jack locked the door with a few last words of comfort. 'Don't worry, Ice, we'll find him.'

He hoped it was true – that Hathor would track down where Seth had imprisoned Ozzy, if indeed that was what he had done. It was still a day and a half to the summer solstice, the Day of Ra, and Jack had the feeling that Ozzy would be held until then to fulfil some purpose of Seth's, and not a moment longer. Once he was no longer necessary, Seth would kill Ozzy as he had attempted to do before – only now, with Ozzy's crown missing, he might find the job a bit easier.

On the way to dinner he paused before the portrait of his great-grandparents. 'What did you get us into,

Grandpa Jay?' The tall handsome figure smiled down at him as Jack searched the painting for something that might indicate how to use the precious liquid. He wondered if the vial was in Jay's pocket, but it looked as though the breast pocket held only a silver fob watch. Apart from the fact that his hair was quite shiny, like Albie's, there was no sign at all of how Jay, or Granny Dazzle, come to that, might have used the oil. Well, Jack could hardly be expected to oil Ozzy's hair. He didn't even have a whole head.

'Talking of which . . .' said Jack. He loitered next to a nearby mirror, taking in his enormous strapping shoulders and his black wolfy head. It was becoming so familiar to him that it almost didn't bother him any longer, but he was pretty certain it would bother his parents. Breathing in and shifting his focus down to his stomach to fix it, he imagined his boyish face, complete with pimples and hooked nose, and watched, mesmerized, as his muzzle shrank away and paled, and his ears receded down the side of his head into two pink question marks.

He grinned at his reflection. 'Jack's back.' Actually, Jack was always there. Whether he was canine and god-like or human and boyish, he never really felt any different apart from knowing that there were certain things he could do when he was Anubis. Minty was right – he really had to discover what other powers he had and use his full potential.

Right now, though, he needed to get to dinner. He slammed open the dining-room door and took his place at the middle of the table. 'Evening,' he said cheerfully, as Bone pulled back his chair and then shook his napkin out on to his lap in an unusually fussy fashion. Jack looked at him suspiciously – was this more of his 'I hate being a servant' act? But no – Bone was waggling his white eyebrows at the napkin, and when Jack spread it out fully on his lap he found that he was staring at himself – a recent school photo that Bone had ironed on to the napkin. 'Thank you, Bone.'

Bone inclined his head and scurried away, flipping up his coat-tails so that Jack could see he had another photograph of Jack stuck on his bottom. He wasn't sure what comment that was making. Nonetheless, it would be a good reminder for Jack if he started to slip into doggyness. Stare at Bone's bottom and remember you're human, he told himself.

Jack's father tapped the table. 'Bone, where's that

Scotch? Need a drink after this dreadful day.'

Lady Bootle-Cadogan, Jack noticed, was staring intently at her fingernails. Something had gone wrong. 'Dreadful, was it? I've apologized a thousand times, Jackson, but as majority shareholder I had to do it.'

'The spa company went into liquidation, Jack,' boomed his father. 'You know how useless I think a spa is, don't you?' Jack shrugged, then nodded, then looked at his mother and shrugged again. 'Well, just imagine how useless I think thirty-two spas are!'

'Thirty-two spas?'

'That's right. Stacked up in the stables like dominoes, nearly three dozen four-seater spa pools.' Lord Bootle-Cadogan grabbed the glass of whisky that Bone was offering and tipped it into his mouth.

'The weather forecast is for a long hot summer, although the presenter seems to be having terrible trouble with his suns. One of them even looked green. Anyway, spa pools will be popular,' said his mother, glaring at her husband. 'We'll sell them over the Internet.'

'Isn't that what the spa company was doing?' said Jack, then stopped short, wishing he could learn to keep his mouth shut. As the image of his mouth popped into his mind, he suddenly pictured a long, floppy pink tongue dangling from slobbering jaws, and instantly his face began to tingle. Almost as instantly, Bone banged the whisky bottle down next to his father, and as Jack looked up he tipped the silver tray on which it had been standing. There on its underside was a picture of Jack. He took it in for a second and felt his lower face return to normal.

Meanwhile his father was off again. 'That's a very good point, Jack. Maybe they do teach you something at that school – wotsitcalled – Clearly Incompetent.'

'It's Clearwell Comprehensive.'

'The point is,' droned Lord Bootle-Cadogan, 'that the spa company was trying to do precisely that. Sell spa pools. By whatever means it could. And it didn't work, did it, my love?' he barked down the table. 'But that was a business. Are we a business? No! We are a family. A family of note. A family with a position in society, with friends in high places, with . . .'

Don't say servants, begged Jack silently. Bone was standing horribly close to his father, the silver salver still in his hand and murderous intent on his face. Jack interrupted quickly. 'Oh, talking of friends in high places, how did you get on with Prince William?'

'Ah, yes, Wills.' His father spoke about him as if the prince was the dear son he never had, or one he wished he'd had in place of Jack. 'Freddy Shelmardine knows his press secretary. The invitation should be winging its way to William right now.'

'So when will it arrive?'

His father pulled a face and stared at his wife. 'How should I know? How long do letters take by . . . whatjacallit these days . . . snail mail?'

'Weeks,' said Lady Bootle-Cadogan bitterly. 'Maybe months, by the time it's gone round all the staff for a good giggle.'

'But . . . it can't! He has to be here on his birthday, on twenty-first June, and that's just the day after tomorrow.'

'Why?' shouted his father.

Jack jumped. He'd forgotten to mention that bit, and how could he explain it away now? 'I . . . I made him a cake,' he said weakly.

On the other side of the room, Bone made a huge show of flicking out his coat-tails and sitting down firmly on an upright chair. So that's what he thought of Jack right at that moment. Only fair, thought Jack. It was hardly a good excuse for a god, a dog-god,

Anubis . . . oh, the ears. The ears were growing. Jack yanked out the napkin from beneath the table, studied it for a moment until he felt his ears return to the side of his head, then blew his nose in it loudly.

'You're an imbecile,' said his father coldly.

'I think it's sweet. Jack, darling, I didn't even know you baked. Perhaps you could make some cupcakes for the next Lowmount fete?' His mother was gazing fondly at him along the table as Bone made barfing motions into the champagne bucket.

'Or for the great Lowmount spa-bath sale,' bellowed his father. 'Little cakes shaped like fishponds. Free with every spa. There, that should clinch the deal!'

This was getting them nowhere. Jack sighed, and finished his meal in silence, using the argument between his parents as cover to write Bone a note on the back of his napkin: 'Where does Prince William live?'

Bone gave him a withering glance, as if to say, 'You want service and Wikipedia as well?' Jack snatched the napkin back. 'Never mind,' he hissed, then louder he said, 'Mum, may I use the computer?'

'Just for half an hour,' she said, poking viciously at her peach melba. 'I need to do some sell . . . some cellular studies of plants.'

Right. Time to go. 'Goodnight.' He didn't even get a response.

Sighing again, Jack slid away from the table. He'd always wanted a normal family, but not so normal that his parents hated each other and got divorced. Beneath the cold superficiality of their lives, he'd always been sure that his parents were really quite fond of each other, but now they seemed to be unable to get along at any level. Even a civilized dinner was more than they could manage. It was a glum Jack who made his way to the computer, snapping at Roger as the dog snarled at him and morphing momentarily into his doggy self, then adjusting his focus so that he turned back into Jack.

Prince William, it turned out, lived in Clarence House in London. Jack printed off a photo of the building and a map, then wandered off in search of Bone. He found him in the corridor, gazing mournfully at the same portrait Jack had been standing before just a few hours before. At Jack's appearance, Bone straightened.

'It's all right – you don't have to do anything else, you'll be glad to hear.' Jack showed him the map. 'I'm going to go to Clarence House and see if I can talk to the prince myself.'

Bone stared at him, then burst into a pantomime of police cars with flashing lights, and Jack being handcuffed and led away to prison.

'Oh, OK then,' said Jack, exasperated. 'I won't talk to him, I'll just . . . Zip back with him and keep him locked up in the museum until the Day of Ra.'

Well, that's much better, said Bone's sarcastic expression.

This was all very tiring. His parents, Al-Bone – everybody seemed to be sniping at each other and at him. The sooner they got the doomed mood of Seth to lift, the better. 'I'll be off then,' said Jack, and rather than endure Bone's disapproval any longer, he thought doggy thoughts until his head morphed, then shifted the picture of Clarence House into his mind's eye and waited for it to settle.

Boomf! There, he was off, his trajectory whizzing him straight across the dining room between his parents – fortunately they were both too busy ignoring each other to look up – and then out through a wall a metre thick before blurring into a black streak and zooming across roads and countryside towards London. M25. Closer now. M4 into Hammersmith.

Even closer. He wasn't sure what route he was taking, so he just trusted his god-dog instincts and allowed them to speed him all the way to St James's Palace gardens and the imposing square white building he'd seen on the computer. 'Now that would make a good cake,' he said, looking up at the stuccoed frontage.

He'd bypassed most of the gates by Zipping, but still wasn't inside the building. Actually, now he considered it, he hadn't really thought about how to get beyond this point. There was only one thing for it. Visualizing the thick parchment letter and the Lowmount seal, Jack allowed his mind to linger on the address: Prince William, c/o Press Secretary, Clarence House, London.

Just as a searchlight reached out towards him, Jack was off again, straight through the wall and into a morning room. Even though he himself lived in a mansion, he was impressed with the look of Clarence House, so much so that he was almost tempted to slow down and have a good snoop around. Then he Zipped through a conference room, and the memory of Mr Catlow laid out in state on the boardroom table shocked him back into action. He wasn't here to sightsee. There was work to be done.

And suddenly the door marked 'Press Secretary' was powering up to meet him. Hoping fervently that the Press Secretary wasn't working late, Jack passed through the door like a lightning strike and slammed to a stop before a large walnut desk. It was rather like his mother's office, only without pictures of spa pools pinned on the noticeboard. 'In tray,' said Jack, knowing exactly how his mother filed things.

There it was – neatly square on the left corner of the desk. With a quick look around, Jack rifled through the file and quickly came upon the very envelope he'd been imagining. It had been opened with a knife, and as it had come from his own father, at Jack's suggestion, he didn't feel bad about getting the letter out and having a look.

Dear Prince William,
Sir Freddy Shelmardine suggested I
drop you a line. We're having a bally
awful time with these back-pay issues
for staff, and thought that you,
as a fresh young representative of
the ruling classes, might have some

205

sterling advice for us.

Do drop in at Lowmount when you have a moment. You can stay in the Red Suite that was especially commissioned for your great-great-great . . . for Queen Victoria. I've a fine malt or two stashed away which I'm sure we can enjoy over our chinwag.
Yours sincerely,
Lord Jackson Bootle-Cadogan

Well, it was hardly an invitation to birthday tea, but it was better than nothing. But only just; sitting here in the Press Secretary's tray, there was no saying when it would actually reach the prince.

He had to do something. Jack thought for a second, then grabbed a pen and scrawled across the envelope in what he hoped was a grown-up, press secretary-ish way:

'Interesting. Think you should go on 21st June. Oh! That's tomorrow, but I've checked your diary and you're free for the day. Lucky! From your Press Secretary.'

Next he found a photo of Prince William on the wall, pictured the same face lying on a pillow and hoped that his Zip facility could work on the basis of such flimsy images. 'Yes!' he whispered, as suddenly he whooshed backwards through the wall with the envelope clearly clutched in his hand, whisked up two flights of stairs and then headed for an anonymous white door at the end of the corridor. At the door he braced himself – he didn't want to go waking up Prince William in his pyjamas – and somehow managed to stop himself from zooming through into the bedroom. He dropped down and peered through the keyhole. No. Even that felt intrusive. He was just going to have to trust his instincts. He was trusting them more and more every day, and so far they hadn't let him down.

Sliding the envelope under the door, Jack tried to picture it crawling across the floor into a big open space. He didn't know whether that would work, but anything was worth a try. Anything to get this son of royal birth to the Tall Trees in time for Seth's showdown with Ra.

Jack checked his watch. Just after midnight. That hadn't taken too long. Maybe there was time for a little snoop around Clarence House after all. Treading as softly as possible, Jack crept along the carpeted corridor and made his way down the rather impressive staircase. The walls were lined with family portraits, just as Jack's house was, and for a moment he wondered whether 'normal' people had oil paintings of their ancestors at home. Probably just photographs. Maybe not even those – and certainly not going back hundreds of years.

He paused on the second-floor landing before an enormous picture of a man about the same age as his Lord Jay in the painting at home, except that this man was dressed like a girl. He wore blue velvet pantaloons, a floppy velvet tunic (hadn't Jack seen his mother wear something like that for gardening?), a lace collar with frills so big he could have kept his breakfast in there, and beneath it all white stockings and black shiny shoes with enormous great buckles. That had to be ridiculously old; in fact, it looked as though the faint date on the portrait said 1653.

The only part of the apparel that Jack approved of was the hair, which was below the man's shoulders, lustrous and curly, and had a bit of a pirate look about it. Maybe it was a wig. 'Johnny Depp wants his hair back,' he whispered to the painting, noticing how the hair was swept back slightly around the ears. Oh yes.

Pirate indeed. The guy was wearing an earring; dangling from a long and fleshy ear lobe was a gold ring with a pearl on it. Where had he seen that earring before? Jack studied the painting for a long moment, trying to work out what was familiar about it, then shook his head.

The place was so similar to home that it was freaking him out. Time to get back to Bone's cottage, to Egypian artefacts, and to friends who were green, or had hawks on their heads, or spent half their time as a seventeen-year-old from 1922. Back to normality. With a Zip, Jack was off.

19

When he got home all was quiet. He visited the crypt quickly, to see whether the 'team' had gathered there, and then Zipped over to Bone's cottage in search of his friends. Even the cottage was deserted, and Jack was momentarily lost. Surely Bone hadn't stayed up at the Hall? He was in a very strange mood, these days, it was true, but even so, it hardly seemed likely that his friend would be hanging around serving drinks to Lord and Lady Bootle-Cadogan any longer than he had to.

There was only one other place that Jack could think Al-Bone could possibly be. Picturing the room where once he had talked to William Waite, Albie's brother – where he had, in fact, witnessed Will Waite having a heart attack – he Zipped over to the undertakers' cottage. Sliding through the thick stone wall, Jack entered the sitting room. It was as he remembered it only mustier, with evidence of a mouse infestation and a definite air of neglect.

From the room behind him there came the sound of knocking. Seth? No, it was a rhythmic banging, so Jack went out through the door for a change, and then crept around the side of the building.

By the harsh light of a fluorescent bulb Bone was hammering the lid on a large walnut coffin. He looked as though he'd been busy for a while, and the tools of his trade were scattered around the room, which was obviously the 'place of business' for the under-takers.

'That's not my father, is it?' said Jack.

Bone started, smacked his finger with the hammer and made a series of faces that said 'swearing loudly'. Then, after glaring at Jack, he pointed to a piece of shiny granite nearby.

'Oh! You had a gravestone made.' When had he had time to do that? What with racing round snake-ridden forests and serving drinks on trays with Jack's face on them, it was a wonder Bone had even had time to eat his own dinner. 'Gordon Catlow,' read Jack. 'Oh yes. I'd forgotten all about him.'

Bone raised an eyebrow, with a 'well, fancy that' gleam in his eye, and Jack shook his head. 'What about passing him through to the Field of Rushes? We could ask him about the plagues.'

They could do that together, now. Bone appeared to think about it for a few moments, and then he nodded and prised the nail out of the lid. Beneath the slab of walnut, the body of Gordon Catlow had been decently mummified, swathed in bandages from head to toe, little amulets and *shabtis* wrapped into the folds and scattered around the coffin, and a blue-and-gold faience scarab beetle positioned carefully over the heart.

'Could we do it here, do you think? Much easier if I get the scales and the Feather of Ma'at and come back.' It was the least that Jack could offer to do after the work that Bone had already put in.

Again Bone pondered his question, a little surprised, and then nodded slowly.

So Jack flurried off for his instruments, heading back through the graveyard and the crypt to make his way down the museum tunnel. In minutes he was back, and they worked together through the darkest hours of the night so that Gordon Catlow would be passed through to the afterlife before the sun rose at dawn.

Dawn. June 21st. The Day of Ra.

At the moment of passing on, the ghost of Gordon Catlow loomed up suddenly from his body, looking very surprised. Then he looked behind him, towards the rays of sun lighting up the west, and his face broke into a huge smile. With a grateful nod to Jack and Bone, the ghost twisted into a glittery vortex and spun away towards the light. What was through there, Jack wondered, to make them all smile like that?

Bone was watching the ghost wistfully – remembering his brother, perhaps.

'Al-Bone, let's go to the crypt,' said Jack. 'Then you can get Albiefied and talk to me. It's way too quiet in here.'

As soon as he said that it was quiet, the air erupted with sound – a ferocious cawing, followed by a high-pitched wail. 'Ice!' exclaimed Jack.

There was no time to wait for Bone to get out the Daimler, or even the hearse that was parked out front. 'Get on!' shouted Jack. It had worked with the bedroom, maybe it could also work with a funeral parlour.

With a questioning look, Bone hastily slammed the lid back on top of Gordon Catlow's coffin and then launched himself on to the top of it. Remembering that his feet had been on the chalet floor at the holiday park, Jack leaped on too, his canine ears quivering in anticipation of another squawk from Hathor – or from Ice. Then he pictured the crypt door, felt the coffin rip away from the floor, and they set off through the open door and across the paddock outside the undertakers' in a heady swirl. Next second, through the fence. Straight *through* the fence. Then the narrow road, the fields, the cattle grid, and across the edges of the graveyard. Ploughing through gravestones and marble plinths that they simply passed right through as if they didn't exist, in less than half a minute they found themselves coasting up the stairs to the crypt, like surfers catching a wave.

The coffin crashed to a stop and Jack grabbed Bone's sleeve, so that together they continued to Zip through the crypt door, Bone transforming into Albie at the very same instant. The sight that met their eyes was one of the most shocking they had ever seen.

'Oh, that's just not right. Minty, are you being . . . nice?' said Jack. 'Albie, look.'

Al-Bone staggered into him. 'My dear Jack, if I hadn't seen it with my very own eyes I would never have believed it, but it does seem as though our Amentet is doing something rather, well, female, I suppose you might call it.'

It beggared belief. Minty had clearly gathered up Ice from the display cabinet and brought her back to the crypt while Hathor delivered his news, and now she was sitting on Granny Dazzle's sarcophagus beside a distraught Ice, holding her hand and rubbing her shoulders with a very concerned expression in her dark eyes.

The eyes turned on Jack. 'Shut up,' she snapped, the old Minty returning instantly. 'Ice has just had bad news, and it's a good job one of us was here to look after her, and it's a good job it wasn't you, because not only are you useless as a god, you are also useless as a human being.'

'Me?' Jack spluttered. 'That is so not fair! I'm always hanging around giving my mum hankies when she's blubbing.'

'And I too have been known to be incredibly kind and understanding on the odd occasion,' confirmed Albie, looking rather hurt.

Minty regarded them both coldly and then said, 'Anyway, since neither of you is going to ask, the bad news is that Hathor managed to spot Ozzy, and he's not in a good state.'

'Where is he?' shouted Jack, refocused immediately, so much so that he could feel his shoulders growing again, ready to burst forth in godly pursuit of his friend.

'Stand with your heads close together,' ordered Minty, and she beckoned to Hathor who was hovering above her.

Mystified, Jack turned to Albie, shrugged and then put his head down. Albie bent to press the top of his head to Jack's, and as they connected Hathor descended slowly and planted a taloned claw on each of them. Jack flinched, expecting it to hurt – Minty wore a leather skullcap to stop the claws digging in. But then his head flooded with light, and he quickly understood the real reason that Minty wore the cap. It was to disconnect her from the stream of images that Hathor could project by pressing gently into the scalp. From Albie's disconcerted cry of 'Goodness!' he knew it was the same for him too.

The bird's-eye view was curious. Although Jack recognized the tops of the snakey fir trees, having hovered above them himself in the grip of the tree goddess, he found that he was distracted by the very extent of the vista. Without turning his head, Hathor could scan a 180-degree view, and the ground loomed and lurched towards them and away as they passed above the firs, over the chalets where the last few holidaymakers could be seen feverishly packing away their things, through the swags of greenish mist that banked up towards the central building and then cleared through the sycamores and then up, up, all around the holiday park while seeing Hathor in flight, reflected in the glass slopes of the side of the pyramid.

And then Hathor perched on the golden capstone, and it felt to Jack as if he too was poised at the top of the great glass building. Leaning over, Hathor peered down into the depths. It was more or less the same view that Jack had seen from the observation corridor near Mr Catlow's office, but from twice – maybe even three times – as high. Jack clutched Albie's shoulders to stop himself from tottering with dizziness and forced himself to look where Hathor's eye took him.

They were gazing straight down upon the central island, from which the waterfall foamed and the slides and helter-skelters of the wave pool stuck out in various directions, like the face of a clock – on the hour, quarter past, half past and quarter two. Jack felt Albie stiffen and cry out, almost tearing his head away; Jack's hands on his shoulders kept him still.

The pink-tinged waters of the wave pool lapped gently against the central island, but even from here Jack could see that the level was rising. And where was Ozzy? His eyes probed anxiously through the greenery – with his emerald skin, Ozzy would be particularly hard to make out among the leafy palms and banana plants.

And then he – or rather Hathor – found him. He was down below them, so directly that it was almost impossible to see him beneath the glare of the capstone, beneath the tumble of the waterfall, beneath the white marble stone that made up the central island. The waterfall was an illusion – not simply a spout that came straight up out of the pool and gushed straight down again like a fountain, but a ring of water about a metre across that rose in a hundred jets that then arced to one side so they could fall back into the wave pool. In the centre was a cube of glass with a convex upper surface. And inside it, with the dark crater in the crown of his head clearly visible in the glare of the shaft of sunlight, was Ozzy.

He was tied to a crystal chair – a throne – and Jack recognized the same nearly invisible bonds with which Seth had captured Ozzy in the ceiling of the crypt. The flail and hook which were his constant companions were cast aside, out of reach, and Ozzy's face was so sombre it looked to be carved from jade.

'Poor Ozzy,' said Jack.

As soon as he spoke the spell was broken; Hathor lifted his claws and beat his wings as he rose above their heads, and Jack suddenly remembered that he was in the crypt, clashing heads with Albie, and was staring at his trainers rather than down into the whirlpool depths of the glass pyramid.

'I've seen this before,' whispered Albie. 'Something . . . something very similar . . .'

'Great!' That had to be a good sign, surely. 'Then how do we get him out?'

'I . . . I don't know.' Albie was close to tears, and he rubbed his spectacles furiously. 'I ruined it. I don't know. Perhaps there's no way out!'

Jack resisted the temptation to slap him. 'Mate, you're hysterical. Get it together! We have to get him out.'

'But I can't.' Albie could barely speak now, and he

looked almost . . . frightened? Cowed at least. The trio of ghostly relatives had turned up in response to Ice's crying, or possibly Albie's crying. Albie seemed very reluctant to meet their eyes, although their eyes were hardly even discernible – all that could be seen were random disconnected body parts doing odd displays, like dabbing on perfume.

'That water's rising,' said Jack. 'And it's Ra day. If we don't get him out, he'll drown. And I think that's about the nicest thing that's going to happen to him. Not to mention to everybody else – or am I the only one worried about the whole tide of death thing?' Nobody answered him, so he shook Albie by the arm. 'Can you remember what to do?'

But Albie was shuddering as if he had flu, his skin grey and clammy. 'No. I can't. I won't do it again.'

Meanwhile Ice resumed her slow siren of weeping, and Minty went back to her position as chief comforter. It didn't look like either of them was going to be much help.

He'd have to do it himself. The only trouble was, he had no idea how, and the only people – if he could call them that – who seemed to have any clue how to tackle the situation had either fallen apart and couldn't tell him anything, or had been incapable of speech in the first place.

This was going to require all his dog-god powers, and then some.

20

If Albie wasn't capable of making decisions, Jack was going to have to order him around to poke him into action. Ice too. Even Minty. Jack hated having to do it; it went completely against the grain. But he couldn't do this all on his own, despite what everyone seemed to think. And weirdly enough, the only people who might have a clue what to do were the people he least wanted to ask.

His parents.

There was very little time for worrying about it, however, so Jack just rattled off a list of instructions that would keep everybody busy for a while, and might even actually *help*, before dashing off to breakfast with Their Lord- and Ladyships.

'Albie, could you get Mr Catlow out of here? It doesn't seem fair that he should be involved any more. Minty, you said something when we were researching that Ra rhyme about what happens on the day of sun – a printout would be great. Ice, perhaps you and Hathor can fly above the park and keep an eye on what's going on with Ozzy, and don't leave him alone, even for a second. He'll be happier just knowing you're there. And ghostly grandparent types – I can hardly see you or hear you. Can you find some way to help me work out what to do, like . . . I don't know . . . find an interpreter?'

'What are you going to do, Jack?' Albie seemed to have found his voice again, momentarily, but it was laced with that sad bitterness that seemed to have overtaken him since the whole servants' back-pay issue had arisen.

'Breakfast,' said Jack.

'You're getting breakfast, while we're out risking life and limb?'

'No, I need . . .' Albie would never understand if he said he needed his parents' advice. 'I need to get something which I think will help.'

'Right. Cornflakes.'

'No.

'Oh, bacon?'

'No!' yelled Jack. 'Just leave it, can you? And get that mummy out of here!'

Perhaps Mr Catlow was being affected by the atmosphere in the crypt. He was knocking on the lid of his coffin. The next moment a bandaged head smashed its way through the walnut and looked around, perplexed. 'Now why's that happening?' said Albie, distracted from arguing with his friend, much to Jack's relief.

'I think it wants you.' A mummified arm was scrabbling through the broken lid too, pointing at Albie. 'Maybe it's one of the ghosts trying to get through?'

Albie rolled his eyes. 'Minty, while you're getting that stuff off the computer, can you look up walking mummies? I'll get him back to the parlour and put a stronger lid on him.'

Jack checked the rate of the sunrise. 'It must be well after seven o'clock. I'll get the things I need, and then everyone meet at the Tall Trees car park at ten. OK?'

There was a murmur of reluctant consent, and the crypt emptied of bodies and spirits. Jack Zipped through to the museum, looking around for something that might serve as his decoy. The only thing that caught his attention was the tent, and that was because the sunlight had followed him down the tunnel from the crypt and was streaming across the room in a solid shaft, so thick it resembled Albie's fighting stick. He checked in the tent: nothing. It was so sad to see it empty of Ozzy and Ice that Jack took to his feet immediately, pausing only to watch his reflection change from Doghead to boy, in the breastplate of a particularly well-polished coat of armour.

The topic couldn't have been more fitting for the dining room. Jack skidded through the door as the grandfather clock in the hall struck eight o'clock, to find his father glaring at his empty plate and his mother sighing like an accordion with holes in it.

'Oh, it's you,' said his father, disappointed. 'Thought you might be Bone. First time in fifty years he hasn't brought me my breakfast. Has he finally died, do you think? He'd better not have. I've warned him . . .'

Lady Bootle-Cadogan heaved another broken breath from the other end of the table. 'Jackson, nobody's expecting you to go and butcher the blessed pig, or even cook the bacon yourself. Just get up off your well-padded behind and get your own breakfast from the buffet . . . over there.'

The sideboard was no more than an arm's length away, but Jack's father was still aggrieved. 'But that's the crux of it, wife! You don't keeps dogs to bark yourself, do you?'

The dog in Jack wanted sorely to interrupt, but his mother had got there first. 'I have a name, Jackson! A name! And so does your son, and so does Bone, and so does every person who's stuck around here for donkey's years trying to keep the place going. Why don't you . . . appreciate us?'

As she grabbed a napkin to blow her nose Jack put down his butter knife. 'I wanted to ask you about that, actually,' he said.

'What, why I don't appreciate you?' snapped his father.

'No, about Bone's name. Did you know that . . .' He'd have to be careful here, or else he could turn the whole thing on its head. '. . . that Bone has discovered that he's actually descended from the Waite family, from when they were the Cornthwaites?'

His mother stopped sniffing in her surprise. 'The undertakers? How on earth did he find that out?'

'Internet,' said Jack quickly.

'Ah, those genealogy sites are marvellous.'

'And not only is he the last living relative, he's actually a trained undertaker.'

Lord Bootle-Cadogan stared suspiciously at the distant bacon platter. 'Hang on. Are you about to tell us that Bone has inherited the undertakers' cottage?'

It seemed to be working. 'And the business,' said Jack. 'Which is good, really, as we don't have an undertaker in the village right now, and there are always people, you know, dying.'

'But he's our servant,' said his father, bewildered. 'He's been with us forever. He fed me toast soldiers and boiled egg when I was sick, and he drove me to Eton, and he's . . . He can't go. He just can't.'

Jack watched, stunned, as his father suddenly shot over to the buffet table and loaded a mound of bacon on to his plate, his back oddly hunched. It sounded rather like gruff Lord B-C was actually going to . . . to miss Bone if he disappeared from their lives. His mother obviously thought so too; getting up quietly, she helped herself to a boiled egg and then slipped it on to her husband's plate.

It was now or never. 'So that's what I was going to ask you, you see – whether Bone isn't actually more of a family friend than a servant, really, and if he's a family friend, wouldn't we want him to do something that makes him happy, and if he moved into the undertakers' cottage he could be independent and still close by, maybe even close enough to stop by . . .'

'At breakfast time?' said his father in a small voice.

'I'm sure he'd miss it too,' said Jack kindly.

'Well, it's only so I can get my hands on that retainer's cottage,' said Lord Bootle-Cadogan gruffly. 'Although what we'd do with the tiny place I don't know.'

'I've got an idea about that,' said Jack. 'You just have to give me a few hours.'

And now to what was *really* the crux of the matter. 'So if that's how we treat the staff, like family friends who've stood by us, what do you think Prince William will say? When he comes to lunch today . . .' he added hopefully.

'Oh, Jackson, is he coming?' squealed Jack's mother.

'I'll call his office. Let's hope so. It'll do the serv— the staff good to see us with the young fella, with his modern ideas.'

Jack eased out of the room. That was two matters dealt with: how to handle other people without coming across all 'lord and master', and how to get a son of royal blood to be there at lunch. Now there was just the small matter of how to get the son of royal blood to Tall Trees.

Wasting no further time, Jack Zipped to the school gate and rested gratefully against the sycamore tree, then jumped up when it rustled above his head. 'Sorry, forgot you were a tree goddess. Is Minty coming? You'll have a good view from up there.'

'Amentet appears beyond,' whispered the tree.

Moments later, Minty appeared, clutching a sheet of paper. As she passed out of the school gates a dark shadow plastered itself across the light of Ra in the sky, and a shower of rain began to patter on to the tarmac behind her. 'I've just sent an email saying I'm absent today,' she explained. 'Probably better if registration hasn't happened yet. Here.'

Jack scanned the printout she'd given him. 'That's right: the Nile will rise and become fertile and all the fruit will come out and so on. What are the diagrams?' Beneath the neat print there was a picture of two pyramids with the sun shining above them. 'Someone in the pyramids shooting at the sun?'

'No, idiot. The sun is entering the pyramid. Some of them were made with shafts and tunnels and mirrors within, so that when Ra blazed on the solstice, these shafts of light would appear. Like laser beams.'

Like the shaft that had appeared from the tunnel behind him and lit up the tent. Jack looked again at the picture. One of the pyramids had a light beam penetrating it at an angle, as if it was going through the side of the building and into its heart. The other was directly below the sun, which sat high in the sky, the shaft of light spearing its way down through the pyramid, directly down, the same way that Hathor's bird's-eye view had targeted Ozzy earlier, through the capstone on the pinnacle.

And suddenly Jack gasped. 'I know what's going to happen. Ozzy's directly beneath that capstone. At noon the sun will blast down through it and form one of these . . . these shafts . . .'

'Part of his head is missing,' said Minty.

'And he's under a glass lens, so it will burn like crazy.' The image in Jack's mind was horrible. 'It will go straight into his head – through uncrowned Osiris of the Earth, like the rhyme said.'

'And none can stem the tide of death, Except a son of royal birth,' recited Minty. 'Is the prince coming?'

Jack could only shrug. He didn't know. But it seemed like their best chance. How could they stop that shaft? How? He needed to find out the way to use that anointing liquid. If only he could talk to Granny Dazzle. If only.

But they couldn't come to him. Of that he was sure. So there was only one option left.

21

Albie was brought back to life by the insistent shaking from a pair of small, brown hands. 'Master Cornthwaite! Master Albert, pleeeeeeease,' begged the young voice. 'Adjo is here. Adjo will save you. Do not please be doing the dying.'

Sitting up slowly, Albie brushed dust from his cracked spectacles. 'It appears I am not doing the dying,' he said slowly. 'Unless . . .'

Unless he was dead already. After all, he had been standing on a statue the size of a small mountain when it shattered into glassy shrapnel and plunged him into an underground lake. And Adjo – how was he? Albie stared at him through his one remaining lens. The boy was covered in dust and had turned a uniform shade of khaki brown, just the whites of his enormous eyes gleaming through the beige. He looked like a sand dune. Well, Adjo had been drowning – of that he was sure – so maybe they were both dead. It was certainly as hot as hell in here.

Adjo peered into his face and then let out a stream of Arabic too quick and joyous for Albie to follow. 'Oh, Master Cornie,' he yelled, mixing up Albie and Cornthwaite in his excitement. 'We are neither of us doing the dying! I think I am dead for sure under the water, because it is sucking me under towards the great statue, and you – you! You stand on top of the great statue, where you have floated like a god to the top of a pyramid, Allah be praised, and all at once: POOOOMF!' Adjo waved his hands around frenetic- ally. 'Everyone is exploding! You, and the great statue, and the coffin on which you are sitting all going BOOOM. Ah!'

For some reason Adjo found this all very amusing, and he sat chortling to himself with tears tracing a streaky path down both cheeks as Albie clambered to his feet and looked around slowly. The ground beneath his feet was how he imagined the surface of the moon might look, dusty and sparkly, corrugated in great unyielding ridges that stretched as far as the eye could see. It wasn't quite sand, but they were evidently outside in the open air; above was the Milky Way, a twinkling road through the sky, so clear it looked close enough to touch. Perhaps they were on the moon. Perhaps not. Adjo must have dragged himself out of the watery depths, grabbed Albie and somehow got them both to safety. 'Where are we?' he asked eventually.

'In the hall of the sucking water and the great statue, Master Albert.' Adjo spoke as though it was completely obvious. 'Except the water and the statue – POOOOMF! They vanish.'

It hurt to breathe in. Albie groaned as he stared around, uncomprehending, his every bone aching with loss and dread. It couldn't be. It just couldn't. He had discovered an enormous, water-filled cavern, the size of the Coliseum, with the echoing emptiness of St Paul's . . . a temple, an edifice, hidden for thousands of years, the Eighth Wonder of the World. A Wonder that he, Albert Bartholomew Cornthwaite, had found all by himself. He was going to be famous. He would be wealthy. He might even be knighted, become Jay's equal . . .

But now there was nothing. Green marble and onyx pulverized in the explosion, so that it would be impossible to distinguish from all the other sand in the desert. Limestone walls crumbled into the floor so that the whole area was now exposed to the elements, as open to the sky as the banks of the Nile. Light-water beams eradicated, and not just the shafts of water – all the water had completely disappeared, along with a building-high statue, and a fragile-looking coffin that was capable of godly transformation.

Everything was obliterated: Osiris's resting place; Lord Jay Bootle-Cadogan's dreams, and the freedom of one young undertaker, Albert Bartholomew Cornthwaite. The only item to have survived was a half-buried shard of ancient wood that once bore the name of a god, the word for 'treasure'. Now the O was broken away and it looked like a ship's title: ADJC.

Albie groaned softly as he withdrew it from the sand. He wasn't dead, but he might just as well be.

The sun was rising as they entered the township, heading for the Oasis Orchid.

'Hail to thee, Ra, at thy rising; at thy rising in beauty, O Ra,' said Adjo solemnly, his eyes on the golden orb. 'He has passed through Duat on his boat and makes his appearance again today.'

Albie snorted. It would be far better for him if Ra hadn't bothered getting up this morning. Anything would be better than having to find Jay and deliver his news.

'Adjo,' he said quietly, 'you must never speak of what you saw in the cavern.'

'But, Master Albert, we were saved by a miracle!'

'No,' said Albie curtly. 'I was about to be involved in a miracle, of that I'm sure. But I interrupted it to make sure you were all right, and then the miracle ended. It's finished forever, Adjo, don't you see? And it would be cruel to tell people of something they can never have. More than cruel – it would be stupid. We would be laughed at.'

Adjo's brown eyes grew rounder, his face stern. 'Oh, I am not liking being laughed at.'

'Nor am I,' said Albie. 'And Lord B-C – he's going to be very, very angry.'

'Oh,' moaned Adjo. 'I am not liking Lord B-C very, very angry.'

Albie sighed. 'Nor am I, Adjo. Nor am I.'

22

Ten a.m. Jack stared above him as he left the Hall with barely enough time to make the rendezvous in the car park. Time hardly seemed to matter any longer. The weather was more important – it had gone bananas. Angry streaks of black and grey banked above his head in a pattern that reflected the crenellated roof of Lowmount – castles in the sky, thought Jack, although these buildings looked as though they'd house violent armies of warring gods, instead of a few elderly National Trust ladies.

In the distance, the swirling skies seemed to be spiralling around a central point. If it had been reaching from the sky downward, Jack would have said it was a tornado, but this funnel was inverted, spinning up into the clouds to a weak spot of sunshine above, watery and pale. Hardly a day for Ra to be proud of. And Jack had a very clear idea of what lay beneath the column of stormy cloud cover.

'Time to go.' Stepping to the side of the doorway so that nobody would see him, Jack focused briefly on his dog features and transformed. It was getting easier. The more he let the image play around in his head, the quicker his altered state came upon him. In just a few seconds his jaw and nose extended, his ears slid up and out, and Jack felt his shoulders burst through his shirtsleeves. He was ready.

A moment for the focus in his mind to shift, and then . . . car park! Zip! He was off, sliding at high velocity through the ornamental gardens, past a bemused gardener who was weeding out the mint in the vegetable rows and straight out across the carp lake and the surrounding fields. It was a slightly new route, going directly from the Hall to the car park, and Jack would have liked a little longer to follow some rather fascinating new smells – badger, if he wasn't mistaken, and something warm and exotic, like alpaca. But time and the clouds were pressing, so he applied his efforts to getting to the car park as quickly as possible.

As the edge of Tall Trees Holiday Park swung into view, Jack judged his distance carefully. Too quick and he might overshoot the car park and end up in the snakey pines beyond. Too slow and he'd never get to the car park in anything like the time he needed. More specific – that was what he needed. A more specific image of where he wanted to end up. He carefully produced a mental snapshot of Bone, Minty and Ice grinning at the back of the VW camper van, like a photo of the weirdest family ever, about to take off on a camping trip.

Just as he was about to laugh out loud, Jack veered into the car park and swooped up to the waiting group of people. They weren't actually near a camper van, but leaning anxiously on the back of the undertakers' hearse. Bone was flourishing his fighting stick in nifty figures of eight; it swished past Jack's face as he screeched to a stop before them.

'Steady! Watch the nose,' he shouted, grabbing the end of the stick.

Bone wrenched it out of his hand and clicked a fingernail on his watch face.

'OK, OK, it's ten past ten, but I'm here now.'

'That's right, he's here now,' bellowed Minty sarcastically. 'Jack will save the day. Clear the way, Jack's here. Let the lord and master through . . .'

'What is wrong with you all?'

Everyone seemed to be excessively wound up. Ice was braced in the hearse doorway, hyperventilating, and Minty's scowl was so deep she looked like a gargoyle. The expression wasn't helped by Hathor, who was kneading her head like a cat so that her scalp shifted up and down, her brow forming thick, wavy lines across her face. Without warning, Minty suddenly swiped a meaty fist at Hathor and the bird tumbled from her head, squawking miserably.

'You asked for it,' she hissed.

They were losing it. Everyone around him was completely falling apart. Jack could quite understand why too – the heat building up beneath the black cumulonimbus clouds was unbearable, and even as he fought it, all nice friendly thoughts were being forced out of his own mind and replaced with evil cotton wool. While they were standing there a fork of lightning skewered through the trees, shooting a fireball in their direction. Hail and fire – well, here was the fire; no doubt the hail would be close behind. Sure enough, icy chips the size of golf balls began to rain down.

'This is Seth again,' he groaned. 'We've got to get to Ozzy. This is how it will always be, for everybody, and that's on a good day. Tide of death, everyone – remember? Let's focus.'

Bone held up a finger. Trotting to the edge of the car park, he thrust the stick into the undergrowth; immediately a shower of asps rained down from an overhead branch.

'There's no way we'll make it through the pines,' said Jack. 'I'll just Zip directly into the pyramid.'

Minty scowled even more ferociously as hailstones glanced off her leather skullcap. 'Hathor's had a look. The whole pool area is booby-trapped with Seth's poisonous green gases, and there's no saying what's underneath them.'

'There is no point, in any case,' wailed Ice. 'Ozzy's missing crown has not been found, the way of the anointing liquid has not been found, and Ozzy's chance for surviving the ray of Ra has not . . . been . . . found.' She shrieked the last word with such anguish that a small flurry of snow joined the hailstones which fell from the black clouds above them.

Jack's spirits were falling rapidly too. They were right. They were all right. Who knew what he would encounter if he tried to Zip straight into the pyramid? It seemed like there was no way through the wave

241

pool, or even the pines before the wave pool, and no way to help Ozzy even if they managed to get to him before noon and the height of the sun – the pinnacle of Ra.

'Granny Dazzle and Lord Jay know how the perfume stuff works,' he said. It was the only hope left. 'We have to find out from them. Then at least there's a faint chance of helping Ozzy.'

'And how exactly do you plan on doing that?' Minty glared at him scornfully. 'They're ghosts, in case you hadn't noticed.'

'I know,' said Jack. He had the beginnings of a part-formed plan, but time was pressing, and nobody else was even trying. Al-Bone was so outraged at everything Jack said at the moment that he seemed incapable of rational thought, let alone any decent sort of ideas as to how to dethrone a nasty pig-god. Minty and Hathor appeared to be bickering, and Ice was intent only on getting to Ozzy. Jack would do it himself, as he'd dreamed up when he'd been talking to his parents. 'They can't come here. So someone has to go to them.'

Bone must have misunderstood him. Suddenly Jack found himself bundled into the back seat of the hearse, and it screeched away with a dumbfounded Jack claw-ing at the window. 'What are you doing? Where are we going?' When he saw the sign for Lowmount he realized what Bone was up to. Trying to help, he clambered around to grab the wheel and Zipped them to the crypt, only to have Bone fighting him off so that the Zip trail veered dangerously along the disused moat and through a sheep pen before sliding to an awkward halt, half in and half out of the crypt.

The front half was inside, however, so Albie appeared. He leaped out of the car and hauled Jack from his seat.

'Oh,' he said furiously, rounding on Jack so suddenly that he had to leap over the circling stick to avoid being taken out at the knees. 'Oh! So somebody has to go and talk to your dead great-grandparents, and I suppose that someone will be me. OK. Fine. Not enough that I almost nearly died already trying to save him, and do all his dirty work. No. Now I have to go talking to dead people – is that it?'

Jack waved his hands in Albie's face, saying, 'No. Listen. No. Listen,' until Albie finally stopped ranting long enough for Jack to speak. 'I'm going,' he said. 'Seeing as I'm Anubis and all that, and can probably get in and out of the underworld a bit more easily.'

Albie stared at him as if he couldn't quite believe his ears. Then, 'Oh no,' he said. 'Oh no, you don't. All my life – lives – I've been investigating Egyptian mythology. I found the resting place of Osiris – and gave Jay the only surviving remnant of it from the coffin, and he threw it in my face. Yes, in my face! And all because I stopped to rescue a little boy, just like you did with Joseph. It ruined everything for me – everything. Only it didn't ruin everything for you, did it, little Lord B-C? And now there's a chance to get to see the Field of Rushes *for myself*, and you think I'm going to let you go and grab all that glory for yourself. Just because you're already a god! Isn't that enough? Isn't it?'

'You're completely bonkers,' said Jack. 'You do realize what you'd have to do to get to the afterlife, don't you? Or put it this way: would you rather . . . die and risk never coming back, or let me go with a very strong chance I can help?'

'Die,' said Albie with a sneer.

'No way,' said Jack, squaring up to him. 'I'm going.'

'You're not. Not again. I'm going,' shouted Albie

furiously, and to Jack's amazement he took a swipe at him with his fighting stick. Jack parried and Zipped out of the way, straight through Albie's body and out behind him, where he spun round and gripped Albie in a headlock.

'You've gone mad,' said Jack as Albie struggled in a frenzy, chucking out punches and digs with the stick in whichever direction he could.

'At least let me come with you!' screamed Albie. 'Treat me like your equal, why don't you?'

But Jack had no intention of taking anyone with him, because he had no idea if he was actually going to make it himself. And even if he did, could he get back? The only thing he was sure of was that he was going to have to take drastic measures. Even going as Doghead might not be enough.

There was no time for this. Clutching the still flailing Albie around the shoulders, Jack Zipped them back to the car park. 'Sort Bone out, will you, Minty? He's lost the plot.'

As Minty cracked her knuckles grimly and then set about wrestling Bone into a vacant coffin that had fallen from the back of the hearse, Jack beckoned to her hawk. 'Hathor, I need to get up high. I want to

245

get above the glass pyramid,' he said. 'Could you lift me out of the trees?'

The great hawk cocked its tawny head at him and looked him up and down, as if gauging Jack's weight. Then with a gentle caw, Hathor positioned himself above Jack's head, seized a shoulder in each taloned foot and beat his enormous wings so that they quickly rose above the roof of the hearse, straight up towards the ominous seething skies and out of the reach of the snake-spitting pine trees. As they drifted up in a steady spiral, Jack focused all his efforts on what he needed to do next, picturing his pink beaky nose in place of the black one.

But Hathor was tiring, and they dropped to only just clear of the treetops. If he had to let go, Jack would find himself plummeting into their midst, to be set upon by a swarming mass of snakes. Even now the branches were brushing against the soles of his feet. 'Ice . . . !' he called desperately, hoping she'd hear him over her own desperate wailing. 'Ice, raise your sisters!'

In response there came a plaintive cry; just as Jack feared he was about to be released he felt the sharp prickle of pine needles being replaced by the tickle of something softer, and Hathor was able to let him drop gently into the hand of one of the sycamore tree goddesses.

'Hello, Sycamore Sister,' he said cheerfully, glad to be well out of the way of the Seth-infested pines. 'Can you hand me on to whichever of you is tallest?'

'As you wish,' whispered the startlingly Ice-like face that appeared from the uppermost branches.

Hand to hand, branch to branch Jack travelled, getting ever higher above the ground, and ever closer to the glass pyramid. Hathor flew beside him, tracking his movements with little turns of his head. When they had the pyramid clearly in their sights, Jack reached out a hand to the hawk. 'Have you got the energy for one last lift?'

With a soundless beat of his beautiful wings, Hathor swooped around and got a firm grip of Jack's shoulders. The next moment he was hoisted clear of the tree goddess and was rising up above the glass slopes of the pyramid, his reflection masking the sight he knew lay below him – Ozzy, trapped in helpless torment in a cube of glass.

'Ozzy.' The image of his friend refocused Jack's mind quickly. 'OK, Hathor.'

Jack held his breath, hardly able to believe what he was about to do. OK, so he was mostly sure that he was immortal. But he wasn't at all sure whether Anubis could operate in the afterlife. Or whether he'd be able to talk to his grandparents, if he was still a god and they were still ghosts.

No. There was only one thing for it. Jack waited until they were almost at the capstone, hundreds of metres above the ground, the wave pool seething and grey with frogs and insects, tinged with red, looking almost alive; the rancid green gasses of Seth's presence snuffing out the effervescent light of Ozzy. When he was sure that no human could survive the fall, Jack said in a slightly shaky voice: 'Drop me, Hathor. Drop me!'

And then as Hathor circled away and Jack plunged through the glass pyramid, Jack imagined himself falling. A boy. A boy falling. Just a boy.

23

Jay appeared to think it was a joke. Or perhaps he was laughing because he'd had a full night of carousing and now appeared slightly deranged, babbling about hearts on strings and finding the dazzle of his life.

Albie sent Adjo to get sweet, hot coffee from one of the traders in the souk and sat his friend/employer down on a low wall. 'Jay, you really need to concentrate. This is critical.'

'What can be critical at a time like this, dear boy?' Jay swayed precariously on the wall. 'I have found true love, and my true love has found me and given me her heart,' and he waved a golden locket around in Albie's face. 'What could be more important than the fact that I am to be . . . married!'

Albie felt a twinge of irritation. So while he had been risking life and limb dragging coffins around the catacombs, Lord Bootle-Cadogan had been flirting and arranging to marry the first unsuitable girl he came across. No, that wasn't fair – Diselda Carruthers was worthy of any man's attention, although Albie wasn't sure how Jay's family would feel about the wedding. But still, was this how it was always going to be? The working classes working, the ruling classes . . . ruling. Albie sighed. With what had just happened, any chance of escaping the working class had probably just eluded Albie forever.

'Drink this,' said Albie, handing Jay the demitasse of strong coffee. 'And do listen, please. This is going to be hard enough to say even once. I'm not sure I'd be able to repeat it. I . . . I took the coffin into the catacombs . . .'

By the time Albie had finished his story, with Adjo standing behind him nodding at intervals to confirm that everything he said was true, Jay looked very sober indeed. He smoothed his moustache with a trembling hand and fixed Albie with his bloodshot eyes. 'So let me be sure I understand this . . . underground cavern . . . Abydos . . . statue of Osiris which was possibly also the fountain of youth . . . coffin in renewal on its way into the statue . . . and now it's all . . .'

'Boomf! Vanish,' said Adjo.

Albie couldn't bear Jay's silence, so he offered him the only thing left from the decimation of Abydos — a small nameplate bearing a few carved letters: ADJC. 'Forgive me, my friend,' he said slowly.

Jay's gaze lingered on Albie's broken glasses. He looked very much as if he would like to smash the other lens to pieces too. Then he let out a deep sigh, and threw the nameplate back at Albie so it fell and lay accusingly in the sand between them. 'I'm not your friend, Albert,' he said stiffly. 'I'm your employer. You were brought out here to do a job, to help me fulfil a lifetime's ambition, and you have . . . you have destroyed it. You will owe me, Cornthwaite. Forever.'

'No,' said Albie. He could stand anything, but not this coldness from the man he so admired. 'That can't be, Jay. It was there, I promise you, we both saw it. We can dig again. We'll start today.'

But Jay had washed his hands of him. 'I don't have the heart to start again. We're done. I'll stay here to get married, and then Diselda and I will travel back to Lowmount. You,' he said with a dismissive flick of the hand at Albie, 'should go home.'

'I don't want to,' said Albie.

'What you want is of no consequence,' said Jay coldly. 'Go home. That's an order.'

He had only one more job to do, and that was another of Jay's orders. Since enough people had noticed that their entire dig had collapsed into the ground, Jay had put it about that robbers had caused an explosion and that in the ensuing disturbance he – Lord Jay Bootle-Cadogan – had discovered what he believed to be the coffin of Osiris.

They posed for a stiff photograph as an ordinary coffin was winched out of a nearby tomb. 'Jay,' said Albie under his breath, 'they'll do tests. They'll realize the truth.'

'I don't care,' muttered His Lordship, smiling grimly for the photographer. 'I want just one moment of glory from this whole sorry debacle. You're not going to ruin that for me too, are you?'

Albie couldn't even speak. How could Jay imagine that any of this was what he would have wanted? True, he had, for a few heady moments, got a little carried away with the thoughts of the fame and glory that might come his way because of the discovery of the statue of Abydos, but he'd never, ever intended that Jay should be given less than his fair share of credit. Jay was the reason he was here, for goodness sake!

He'd been so proud. So delighted to be chosen above his older brother and given this amazing opportunity. And now it was all in ruins. Clearly Jay thought of him as nothing more than a servant, and an ungrateful one at that.

But about one thing Jay had been right. Albie did owe Lord Bootle-Cadogan. Forever.

So, later that evening, when his former friend turned up in the doorway of Albie's room and cast a disparaging eye over his trunk, Albie lied for the first time in his life. 'I'm on the first boat in the morning,' he said.

Jay shrugged. 'I'm not sure when we'll be back. We'll be married on Wednesday, and then we'll take some time for a honeymoon, and wend our way back to Lowmount some time after that.'

'Would you like me to say anything to your mother?'

Jay inspected the door frame carefully. 'No,' he said after a while. 'Thank you. What I'd really like, Albert, is for you to stay out of my way for a very long time. If I ever need to call on your services again, I'll let you know. Goodbye.' Jay stomped away down the corridor, blowing his nose into a large laundered handkerchief.

'My . . . services?' It was as if he'd been kicked in the gut by Jay's shiny brogues, shoes that he himself had polished on so many occasions. So this was his only role in life. A servant.

Well, he wasn't going to be treated like that ever again. Tipping his trunk out of the open window into the cart waiting below, Albert Cornthwaite vowed that he would reinvent himself, some way or other. He would prove to Lord Jay Bootle-Cadogan that he was any man's equal.

24

'Jack,' said a familiar voice. His mother? No, someone like that but not her . . . someone . . . 'Jack, come on. Open your eyes.'

He definitely knew the voice, and he knew the eyes that gazed into his when he did finally open his own. But they were different to how he'd last seen them. 'Granny Dazzle,' he said blearily. 'Your eyes aren't wrinkly and baggy.'

'How nice of you to notice,' said his great-grandmother. She smiled at him, and Jack stared. She had nice white teeth too. No wrinkles, and nice little white teeth, and rather a daring dress on, and legs in white stockings . . . eugh. Granny Dazzle's legs. Eugh. He'd never even spotted that she had legs before . . .

'You're young,' he said, confused.

'Just a few years older than you,' said his dazzling great-granny. 'And here's Lord Jay.'

An enormous hand wrapped itself around Jack's fist, pumped it up and down a couple of times and then in the same action hauled him to his feet. 'Darned audacious move, Jack my lad,' boomed a deep voice somewhere high up. 'Might have died of shock if I wasn't dead already.'

'Lord . . . Jay . . . um . . .'

'Great-Gramps,' said Lord Jay warmly. 'I can't believe we finally meet face to face.'

Jack checked his body over, starting with his face. He was still a boy, and felt solid enough to not be a ghost, but Lord Jay's hand had been fairly human-feeling too. 'So I . . . I did it!' he whispered.

Granny Dazzle's youthful eyes filled with tears. 'I can't believe you'd do that, Jack. What an enormous risk.'

'Well, it's a bit of an enormous problem, to be honest,' he said with a shrug. He'd had no idea whether it would work, only that his powers as a dog-god weren't developed enough to get him to the afterlife, where he needed to be. The only other way he could think to get there in a hurry was to do what everyone else had done who was already there, which meant that he had to . . . had to . . .

'So am I . . .' Lying in a mushy mire of blood on the floor of the pyramid, he wanted to say, but it didn't seem quite the thing to say to great-grandparents . . . 'Am I in the right place to find out about that perfume?'

'Yes!' said Granny Dazzle, but Lord Jay laughed.

'Hang on a moment there, old chap. There are one or two people around here who'd like to meet you first.'

For the first time, Jack looked around him to see where he'd actually ended up. He appeared to be in a ballroom, but the ballroom at Lowmount would have fitted into this one a thousand times over. With golden columns, glittering facades and faience and jade jewels inlaid in vast, endless walls, there was splendour in every direction, as far as Jack could see.

And it was full of people.

The first to grab him was a Lord Jay lookalike with enormous floppy ear lobes. He seized Jack's hand and squeezed it into a banana shape. 'Good man, Jack Algernon. I'm your granddaddy.'

Jack was having trouble keeping his eyes off the swinging ear lobes. 'You're . . . Johnnie! Hi . . . hello . . . oh!'

A short man had barged Johnnie out of the way and thwacked Jack on the shoulder with a stumpy hand. 'Thank you, sir, for moving us on. Been in that graveyard forever, it felt like. Percy the gardener.' Percy touched his cap, and then pointed out the lady behind him. 'Mrs Percy's very grateful too.'

'Oh, I am, sir. We didn't want endless torment.'

Jack laughed. 'No, well, who does? Ah, Will! Hello!' He recognized Will Waite from when he'd been alive, and also because in the afterlife he looked very like an older version of Albie.

'That's right, sir, William Cornthwaite. This is Mother – Vera.' A grey-haired lady smiled anxiously. 'How's our Albert doing – behaving himself?'

'He's . . .' So much better than that, he was going to say, but then he remembered that Albie wasn't really quite himself at the moment, even when he wasn't being Bone. 'He's great,' he said.

'He was always such a special boy. So much cleverer than me, and with this massive sense of adventure, and loyalty, and . . . oh, you know all that.'

'I do,' said Jack, although he had the feeling Al-Bone wouldn't see it that way.

'Look after him for us,' said William earnestly, and

Jack noticed a slight frown pass across Lord Jay's face. 'Better not hold you up though, sir – all these people want to say hello.'

Jack looked down the line behind him. 'Crikey.' There had to be nearly a thousand of them – every person that he'd helped to pass over to the afterlife by carrying out the Opening of the Mouth ceremony. Mr Catlow was there, giving him a grateful thumbs-up, and Jack hurried over to him.

'Mr Catlow! Your boils have gone!'

'And the extra eighty-two pounds I was carrying,' said Catlow proudly. He was still a big chap with a highly-coloured face, but he looked like a fit and seasoned rugby player instead of a fleshy, lumpy corpse. 'I wanted to thank you.'

'Oh, well, Al-Bone did most of the work.'

Mr Catlow shook his head. 'No, I meant for closing down the Tall Trees before any other deaths occurred. I've been eating myself into an early grave for years, to be honest, so no surprises what happened to me. But those holidaymakers . . . well, they'd paid good money for a great time, and I couldn't deliver, and to think what might have happened! I feel bad about that.'

'Is that why your mummy was trying to escape?'

The man smiled modestly. 'Just trying to help. I thought I might haunt the place to encourage everybody to leave.'

'Seth – the pig – was already doing that. You know you were set up?' said Jack.

'I love it here,' said Mr Catlow with a shrug. 'I'm fit and playing all my sports again; some of my old teammates are here and we're starting up a rugby league. So it doesn't worry me at all. In fact, I wanted to return the favour. Been having a chat with your great-grandparents, so I know a thing or two. When you get back, take the disk from Mrs Sombourne's computer. It will help.'

Jack shook his hand, surprised. How a computer disk might help, he couldn't quite imagine. But the mention of the Tall Trees reminded him why he was there. He stared down the enormous conga-line of people waiting to greet him and add their thanks to Mr Catlow's.

He cleared his throat and addressed them loudly. 'Look, it would be lovely to meet you all, but I'm not quite sure how time works here. I do know it's ticking by for Ozzy and, you know, the rest of that world, so . . .' He grabbed Granny Dazzle by the elbow. 'Is there somewhere quiet?' he hissed.

Diselda nodded. 'Jay, get him through the doors. I'll just deal with this lot and then we'll explain the perfume.'

They left her calming down the disappointed crowds with promises of a singalong later. 'And Cleopatra's promised to kick it all off tonight,' she was calling as Jay led Jack along the back of the ballroom and through a small door lit with the sign of Ra, which was set into the corner of the most enormous pair of doors imaginable. Above Jack's head, a crossed golden flail and hook held the great doors in place.

Lord Jay smiled down at him as Jack stepped through the door. 'This is Osiris's domain,' he said, pointing up at the flail. 'Welcome to the underworld.'

25

Jack wasn't sure if he was actually breathing any more anyway, but at the sight beyond the doors he was pretty sure his heart would have stopped.

It actually looked rather like the dining room where his parents had their daily battles, but on a similar scale to the ballroom. In place of the table was a low golden dais, the length of an aeroplane runway, and then on either side sat three awe-inspiring chairs. No, not chairs, Jack realized. Thrones. Vast, golden and jewelled, each adorned with symbols and hieroglyphs.

'Wow. I wish Albie was here,' he said softly. 'He'd know what they all meant.'

A flash of anguish passed again over Jay's face. He coughed, then said, 'I happen to know too. These are the thrones before which all must pass to get to the Field of Rushes, through those doors at the far end.' Jack felt his nose lifting; even with his boy's head he could smell the most delicious aromas and he knew they came from the other side of those doors. It smelt like . . . like freedom, and joy, and fun. Endless fun. He almost wanted to chase a stick right through those doors. Right now. Well, he was Anubis, after all. Maybe he could . . .

'These are the thrones of Osiris and Isis.' Jay pointed to the grandest of the thrones, which were so beautiful that Jack struggled to look at them. 'Then thrones for Thoth the Recorder, and for Ma'at.'

'Oh! I use her feather in my ceremony,' said Jack.

'Correct.' Jay smiled as he pointed out the two thrones nearest to them. 'This one is for Amentet,' he said, looking at the one on the left. Then he turned slowly to the other. 'And this is for the god of embalming and mummification, the god who makes this whole process possible . . . Anubis.'

Jack stared at the throne. His throne. It was huge, so beyond any measurement that made sense in his world that he couldn't begin to put words to it, and more ornate than anything Jack had ever seen. Just one of the rubies stuck in it would cover all the back pay for the entire Lowmount staff forever and a day.

But more significant even than that was the face embossed into the top of the throne. It was . . . Jack's face.

Doghead.

'I'm supposed to . . . to stay here,' he whispered.

He'd been thinking about it only seconds before – what it would be like to burst out through those outrageously huge and shimmering doors and go and frolic in the Field of Rushes with Mr Catlow's rugby team, with a stick, with his dear, dear Granny Dazzle and his great-grandfather . . .

But then he thought of everyone he'd have to leave behind, and suddenly a lump formed in Jack's throat. He didn't want to stay here. He still had a life as a boy to lead. And yes, being a god was fun and all that, and definitely not boring, but all he'd ever wanted was to be normal, and here was a throne next to the Field of Rushes with his name on it.

He looked at his great-grandfather with panic in his eyes. 'I don't want to stay.'

Jay shook his head, his handlebar moustache quivering. 'Nor should you, Jack,' he said. 'I got the wretched family into this, and I'll make sure you don't have to stay. Somehow. I made such a mess,' he said, 'such a dreadful mess of everything. And when you get back I want you to . . .'

Jack tore his eyes away from Lord Jay's slightly tortured face as his great-grandmother slipped through the golden door to join them. It was so wonderful to see her, and to find her young and so well. There were definite advantages to being a god, but even so . . .

'Jack, you look terrified,' she said. 'Jay, what have you been telling him?'

'Just that he has to go back,' said Jay, raising an eyebrow. Let's keep this between ourselves, Jack, the eyebrow said.

'You do have to go back,' said Granny Dazzle.

'I agree.' He had no idea how to do that, of course, but he wasn't going to worry them with the details. 'So tell me about how to use the perfume.'

'It's not the perfume,' said his great-grandmother. 'It's the bottle.'

'It's an ancient artefact I managed to pick up after Albie and I . . . discovered the resting place of Osiris.'

'The stopper is a sun-channelling device,' said Granny Dazzle. 'If held by a son of royal birth, it will

265

filter the harmful rays away from the head of Osiris.'

'Ah!' It all made sense. The long diamond filament was the key. In fact, Jack could picture it already – if Prince William held it in a certain way the shaft of sunlight would be caught in a prism and diverted, halted on its searing journey into Ozzy's open brain. 'I have to get . . .'

Before he could finish his sentence, an enormous scream rattled through the tiny door behind them. Lord Jay patted his pockets as if looking for a pistol, then he thought better of it. 'No good here anyway,' he muttered.

He ran to the door, with Jack close behind and Granny Dazzle bringing up the rear. As they paused in the doorway, Jack had a horrible feeling of déjà vu. All his lovely ghost friends were shouting and slapping at each other, and from the distant vaulted ceiling of the ballroom a black sheet of rain descended. Asps. The snakes were attacking.

'Not here as well!' he groaned.

'It's a bad sign,' said Diselda. 'They can't harm dead people, obviously, but it's an indication that Seth's getting a grip on matters up above. The tide is turning.'

'The tide of death,' said Jack grimly.

'Go, Jack,' urged his great-grandmother.

He wasn't sure quite how to do it, but if focusing on being a boy had got him into the afterlife, then there must be some way to reverse the process to get out of it. He was god of the afterlife, after all. How would Minty do it? Concentrate. She'd concentrate. So far he'd focused either on being a dog-god or a boy, *OR* on Zipping. Maybe, if he worked really hard at it, he could concentrate on both at once. 'Wish me luck,' he said, giving Granny Dazzle a kiss on the cheek.

'You'll do it, Jack,' she said confidently.

Lord Jay grabbed his hand firmly, and Jack felt something slip between his fingers. 'Tell Albie to check the museum cases for what he gave me. I picked it up when I'd calmed down. I said terrible things and then he never saw me alive again, so that . . . that's for Albie,' whispered his great-grandfather, curling Jack's hand around the object so that his wife wouldn't see it. Then he added, 'Go to it, young man,' in his usual aristocratic bellow.

Jack took a deep breath. They seemed very sure he'd be able to get out of here, so maybe, just maybe, he could. With every scrap of concentration he could summon, Jack pictured his doggy self back in the Tall Trees car park, back with Albie and Minty, back under the darkening skies, back with the portmanteau and the perfume bottle, its mysteries now revealed, and back, hopefully, to where he would drag Prince William once his father had got him to Lowmount . . .

Suddenly the throne room swam around him, the faces of his great-grandparents blurred, and he knew it was working. There was so little time left, it had to be working.

26

Bone looked even more furious than when he'd departed. He loomed over Jack with his stick braced for attack, like a bespectacled Grim Reaper. 'Sirrrrrr!' he bellowed furiously.

'Hathor showed us what you'd done, you blithering idiot.' Minty gave him a prod in the ribs with her toe and Jack realized he was lying in the car park. 'Bone's saying you could have died!'

'That was sort of the point.'

Jack looked around above Bone's head. The sky was no longer like sky at all; it resembled an upturned cauldron of boiling oil, smoking and spitting and illuminated only by one tiny speck of light in the far, far distance. The sun.

'Ra,' he croaked, sitting up. 'What time is it?'

Bone pulled his battered old fob watch from his top pocket and passed it to Jack.

'Eleven forty. Twenty minutes to go. Where's Prince

William?' Scanning the car park and the road that led up to it, Jack hoped desperately for the purr of a royal car, or even the sight of his father, but there was nothing but the threatening howl of the skies above. 'He's not going to make it in time. I have to go and get him.'

Minty grabbed him by the arm and hauled him to his feet in the same action. 'No time, dog-boy,' she said, beckoning to her hawk. 'Hathor can go and look, but we'll have to get over to the pyramid. Ozzy's nearly gone already.'

Bone put back his fob watch and pulled out the bottle in its place. That fob watch. The size of it reminded Jack of something, and he opened his hand to discover what it was that Lord Jay had passed to him. But of course there was nothing. Like the bottle, solid objects couldn't pass between this world and the other.

He stared at the bottle as Bone thrust it at him. Everyone was looking at him questioningly. 'So?' asked Minty, impatiently. 'Did your little brush with death serve any useful purpose? What's the bottle for?'

At least he had solved that mystery. He removed the lid from the bottle and held it up to the dying light so that it was reflected off the facets of the crystal. 'Look! It's not the bottle that's important, it's the lid – it acts as a filter for the sun's rays!'

But even as he said it, he knew it wasn't enough. They only had part of what they needed to save Ozzy – they had the sun-channelling device, but no prince to hold it.

Jack flicked his ears back and forth, desperately seeking a sign that the royal son was on the way. 'But we need Prince William. It won't work without him!'

Even as he said it, and Ice's wailing from the back of the hearse reached fever pitch, Jack knew what they'd have to do. They would have to try anyway. They couldn't just leave Ozzy there without even attempting to do the right thing. What would have been the point of his mission to the afterlife?

'All right,' he said, before anybody tried to persuade him of what he already knew. 'We'll do it ourselves. Minty, you're a god, so that should be some use, and Ice, and me . . .'

Bone looked treacherous again.

' . . . and Al-Bone, you're the only one with any actual knowledge, the only one who's bothered to learn about all this stuff,' said Jack, suddenly angry and sad and despairing for his friend. 'Your brother just told me – you're way cleverer than he was, and adventurous and loads of things. You have to help. No, you have to *lead*.'

Bone shook his head, then bowed low and tugged an imaginary forelock. Servant, he was saying. I'm just a servant.

'Says who?' shouted Jack.

Whatever rage had been pent up in Bone's slender frame was suddenly unleashed all at once. He spun round with the stick in his hand, flourishing it madly, not in any fighting manoeuvre but in an uncontrolled and spiky fashion, as if he had no control over his limbs or his frothing mouth. You say! You do, he seemed to be saying. You and your stupid upper-crust family.

Jack filled with dismay. Al-Bone was having some kind of breakdown, and the timing couldn't have been worse. Furthermore, he seemed to think it was all Jack's fault. All at once Lord Jay's guilty expression flickered into his brain, flashing across his face as his great-grandparents' ghosts tried to make an appearance in the car park and failed, and tried again and were snuffed out like candles, and Jack felt once more for the object that wasn't there. And then he got it.

'Oh, Al-Bone. He cut you out of it, didn't he? Lord Jay – he acted, um, like my father?'

The tears streaming down Bone's face confirmed it. Jack wanted to cry himself, to think that his beloved ancestor could have acted like that. It was a tragedy. Too awful to think about . . .

'He's sorry!' said Jack suddenly. 'Bone, he was trying to tell you how bad he felt, I'm sure of it. He said to check the museum cases for what you gave him, because he picked it up. And he tried to give me something . . .' In a bound he was moving Ice out of the way and upturning the portmanteau on to the blackening floor of the Tall Trees car park. '. . . for you.'

He flung open the portmanteau doors and started casting artefacts and ceremonial gowns aside. The tiny compartments of personal belongings at the back – that was what he needed. Where the spectacles had been stored. 'It didn't transport from the underworld, but I bet it's here, if I can just . . .' Yanking open door after door, he knocked the contents to the floor, and then finally the last compartment yielded its treasure. 'This is it!'

He held it out to Bone, who just looked at it, disappointed. Then he pulled out his own old fob watch, as if to say, 'I've got one.'

'No,' said Jack, sure he was right. 'He tried to give it to me for a special reason, I just know it. Hang on.'

His hands felt enormous and clumsy as he fumbled to open the intricate mechanism that held the engraved silver casing in place. Suddenly he felt a cool hand on his own.

'I can help,' said Ice gently. It was the first time she'd stopped fretting over Ozzy in an age. 'Help I can,' she added with a small smile. And then she blew softly on the clasp; with a tiny *ching!* the casings flew open on either side of the watch face.

Jack read it and smiled, and then handed it to his friend. 'It's definitely yours,' he said. '"For Albert Bartholomew Cornthwaite, Archaeologist and Discoverer" – see?'

Bone read the inscription, blinking rapidly.

Jack grinned. 'There's more, on the inside of the back casing.'

Bone read it, open-mouthed, and then stared at Jack with his eyes over-bright. 'Sir,' he said softly, and

Jack knew he wasn't talking to him.

'Sorry to break up your boy-bonding moment, but what does it say?' groaned Minty.

Jack said it for him. 'It says: "Forgive me, my friend."'

Bone smiled blearily as he unhinged his jaw to speak. 'Engggg,' he said, then shook his head.

'I know. Not sir. Not his servant. His *friend*,' said Jack again. 'Like you're *my* friend. And right now there's another friend who desperately needs your help. Does "tide of death" ring any bells?'

It was as if someone had switched on Bone's power source, and with a beam of light that cut through the darkness of the forest, Albie appeared. 'Come on!' he screamed.

'Jay must have broken the curse somehow,' said Jack. 'Wow.'

Albie looked down at himself, surprised, and then a gleam flashed in his eyes and he pointed his fighting stick into the forest. 'Osiris, I found you once, and I'll find you again!' he roared, and with a quick swoop of the stick above his head, he was off, ploughing through the undergrowth with superhuman strength, the stick circling so fast that tumbling snakes were forced out of it in a spray of little black chunks that fell like coal on the floor of the forest.

'Before he kills himself, I'll buy us some time,' said Minty, throwing Hathor into the air and spinning in a circle. Above her head rain started to fall; as the circle grew bigger the ring of water spread outward, and suddenly Jack was back on the floor of the forest car park, staring up at Albie. This time, however, Albie took one look at him, patted the two fob watches in his pocket, and reached down to help Jack to his feet.

'Sisters!' cried Ice, her dark hair streaming out behind her in the ferocious wind. 'Assist us.'

The ground bucked beneath their feet as the syca-mores beyond the swathe of hostile pine trees ripped their roots from the earth and forged their way across. As if listening to some distant call, Ice grew very still and quiet and then, to their astonishment, she started to grow, taller and taller, her arms and her hair fanning out like the branches of a tree until just Ice's beautiful face peeked out from above the foliage, high up in the sky.

'Scary,' said Albie.

'I sometimes forget she's a goddess as well,' said

Jack in agreement, as Ice the Tree bent to pick them up and then passed them to her nearest Sycamore Sister.

'How much time?' he shouted to Albie.

'Six minutes. No, four! I don't know, these watches are different. Oh, forget it!' roared Albie. He pointed above them as their hand-to-hand journey through the sycamores speeded up and they edged ever closer to the great glass pyramid. 'It's not a precise timing thing,' he shouted to Jack. 'In Ancient Egypt, they would have just relied on the moment when the sun was at its highest and taken that as the moment of Ra.'

'How will we know?' shouted Jack above the tremendous gale. The skies were so thick with black clouds boiling with hailstones and striking streaks of fire that the sun was impossible to see.

'Get in position,' cried his friend. 'You'll know when the time's right. And don't let anything distract you. That's how I lost Osiris last time.'

They were swaying towards the capstone. As Jack looked down he saw with a start that Albie was right. The process was beginning anyway, no matter what time the clock said it was. The golden capstone was twisting away in four different directions, directly beneath the gaping funnel through the clouds, so dark that it looked like a length of black hosepipe, with a winking eye at the far end that he knew was the sun, just edging, nudging its way into position.

Before it fired straight to earth.

Before it fried Osiris alive, and turned the tide towards evil.

Below, far below, a dank green face swivelled towards him, a vicious grin spreading across it in a slimy, gore-filled expression of triumph.

They gazed at each other, Jack's brown eyes meeting the porcine red eyes of the pig-head through the shattered glass panel at the top of the pyramid – the one he'd fallen through, he guessed. It was waiting for him. Waiting to gloat.

'Not yet, you don't,' he said quietly. Then, nudging the Sycamore Sister with his foot, he pointed towards the door at ground level. 'That way,' he said.

27

The tree deposited them at the door through which they'd driven the hearse just a few days before.

'By my estimation, Jack, we have less than two minutes,' said Albie, squinting up through the glass ceilings to where the dark funnel of cloud was creeping ever closer to the capstone, which was opening like a flower in bloom.

'Hathor,' grumbled Jack as they ran along the corridor, 'where are you? Where's that prince?'

They were passing the lifts where previously they'd travelled up to see Mr Catlow's dead body. Jack glanced around him and then beckoned Albie straight on. 'He'll be expecting us to try to get above him to stop the light,' he explained. 'Let's try going in underneath. Maybe we can get Ozzy out of the cube.'

'Plan B,' said Albie. 'I like it.'

The corridor led straight forward, also heading for the very centre of the pyramid but this time at ground level. At the end the ground sloped away and they found their way barred by a pair of large white doors. 'Hang on to me,' said Jack; Albie grabbed his arm and, without even faltering in his running step, Jack pictured the wave pool on the other side of the doors and with a motion as though they were splitting away from time itself, they slid side by side along the rest of the corridor and straight through the thick white barrier.

To their astonishment, they were underwater. Albie spluttered and then glared at Jack as his spectacles drifted away. The doors were obviously service doors for the wave pool, only to be used when the pool had been emptied. Now it was far from empty, as surging and turbulent and oily as the North Sea, with so little light filtering through that it was almost as if they were back in the forest. Why was it so dark?

There wasn't time to investigate thoroughly: even Jack was gasping for breath, although he suspected he might find a way to breathe underwater if he had the wherewithal to focus on it for a while. Albie, meanwhile, was turning a strange rainbow of colours – red from trying to hold his breath, blue at the edges from where he was losing the battle, and green in the reflected glow of the evil pig vapours that swarmed all around them. Grey shadows dappled his cheeks as well, and when Jack peered upward to find out why, he saw something he couldn't quite understand. Feet. Hundreds – no, millions – of little pink feet paddling away above them, blocking out the light, the air, the chance of escape . . .

There was nothing else for it though. They had to go upward – and now. Getting hold of Albie's sleeve just as his eyes were rolling back in his head, Jack struck out for the surface. The thick grey carpet above them broke apart as his head nudged through, and he pulled Albie up into the space and shook him until he heaved in a great strangulated breath. As Jack watched to make sure his friend was still alive, a piece of the grey carpet broke away and lunged at his face, the tiny pink feet clawing at his delicate black dog-nose. Albie stopped breathing again and started screaming instead.

'Rats! O my lord above, it's full of rats. I hate them, get them off me. Jack, get them off me!'

So much for the element of surprise. Jack didn't like rats much either (although somewhere in his canine psyche a surge of excitement pulsed through him – rats! They'd be fun to chase). But he could see why they'd have been attracted to the place: the trails of blood blending into the water seemed to come from the carcasses of dead sheep and cows that floated eerily in the wave pool, rats swarming over them. Diseased livestock. Another plague. Another sign that the tide of death was upon them.

Doggy-paddling madly with his feet, he clamped a hand over Albie's mouth. 'Be quiet! We don't want Seth to know we're here!'

'Fat of a cat!' whimpered Albie desperately.

'Have you gone mad?' said Jack desperately.

'No, according to the Ancients we need fat of a cat to get rid of them.' Albie was so terrified of the seething grey mass that he was starting to sink below the surface again rather than tackle any of the snapping rodent faces that now surrounded them, crawled up them, swam under their collars and down through their clothes, nipping, scratching . . .

'I can see sheep and cows but no cats,' Jack spluttered, 'so we'll have to do it my way. All right, rats,' said Jack suddenly as a large one made a racing dive for his jugular, 'you took on the wrong dog.'

He was severely hampered by Albie's dead weight

as terror froze his friend's limbs, but he couldn't just leave him to sink into the bloody depths of the wave pool. Instead he took up the perfect doggy-paddle position, shoved Albie up on to his back as if he were an inflatable in a swimming pool and then he set off with a surge as he opened his jaws.

The first rat looked as if it was about to swim down his throat. Gross, thought Jack miserably. Then he clamped his teeth shut, trapped the wriggling rat in his mouth and flung it to one side. He might have broken its neck – he wasn't sure, couldn't really bring himself to think about it – but in any case, he realized as the creature flew through the air above the wave pool that it had already been dead when he bit it. Arcing above the stormy waters, the rat disintegrated in a shower of nasty grey sparks and vanished from sight.

'Albie, they're spirits,' he said, gnashing his teeth at a juicy specimen swimming towards him. 'Whack them!'

Not looking terribly convinced, Albie dragged his stick up through the water, pointed it at a nearby rodent, and stabbed wildly, crying, 'Inauspicious! Inauspicious! You should not see any rat on this day.

You should not go near it in your house. This day, on which one wards off all matters of Sekhmet!'

'Sekhmet?' Jack lodged a medium-sized rat on his canines and lobbed it into the air.

'Goddess of Pestilence,' panted Albie, rowing with hefty sweeping motions in either direction through the gap in the slew of rats that his incantation had created.

'See, you do know everything,' said Jack.

Between them they cut a swathe towards the central island. A weak sliver of light was fizzing through the air from the shattered glass near the golden capstone, flickering on and off as if the signal wasn't strong enough. But it was getting close. Even with a face full of rats and Albie riding on his back with his fighting stick, like some water-bound medieval jouster, Jack could see that. Any moment now the sun would click into position. The shaft of its ray would be magnified a kazillion times over along that black tube of cloud. It would reflect the light back into itself, and then down through the capstone, penetrating right to the heart of the glass pyramid, with no golden scarab to protect it, just the evil fetid steam that swirled around Seth's head, ready to move at that same moment.

Jack chucked a rat away and peered ahead. The central island was only metres away now, although the child-friendly tiles and fun tubes and slides were completely obscured by a writhing blanket of rats, and what else . . . oh yes, snakes, swarms of flies, clouds of mosquitoes. It was like a South American jungle.

A malevolent red glow nestled at the centre of the mass of black and dark, dank green – Seth's eyes, smouldering like hot coals, looking out for them.

'We can't go that way,' said Jack, ducking his head down in the water. 'Albie, we're going to have to dive. Give me your naboot.'

Mute with terror at the prospect of sinking once more beneath the sea of rodents, Albie passed over his stick. As calmly as he could, Jack snapped it in half and handed one section back to Albie. 'I'm going to swim under. Use this like a snorkel. I don't know if I'll need it, but I've got the other half just in case.'

Albie closed his eyes in silent prayer, then popped one end of his beloved stick into his mouth as Jack turned tail and plunged below the surface of the wave pool, dodging the scratchy pink feet and snapping teeth that tried to spear his eyes. Now he could see it – the foundations of the island, with windows cut in the side, and behind the windows . . . a sight he could hardly bear to see.

Ozzy was statuesque in his grief. Within the glass confines of the cube beneath the island was a golden throne, just like the ones that Jack had seen in the great hall leading from the ballroom to the Field of Rushes. This one was a shameful mockery of the great thrones of the afterlife, with rough edges, symbols and hieroglyphs depicting Seth in charge, Seth as ruler of the underworld, the newly dead clambering from the Nile looking for solace and being turned away by a sneering pig-faced god, and, worst of all, a picture on the back of the throne of the very event that they were about to see – Osiris, manacled to his throne like a death-row prisoner in the electric chair, his head pinioned upright by a web of snakes that encased his jaw, his neck, his upper torso, and that javelin of white-hot heat slicing its way through Ozzy's head and splitting his noble face in half.

And just as Jack let out a startled cry and Albie spluttered so much that his stick floated up to the surface, they saw what they had dreaded the most: the edge of Ozzy's prison cube was flooding with light, a light so searing and bright that they could hardly stand to look at it, or to watch Ozzy's eyes closing in pain and anguish. Even now he refused to struggle, and Jack was amazed at just how regal his little green friend looked. Regal. Like Prince William. Who wasn't here.

'It's hopeless,' he said into the water, bubbles rising around him as Albie too abandoned his attempts to stay upright and breathing and simply swam to the side of the cube, his hands and face pressed against the glass, tears mingling with the foul waters of the wave pool.

Ozzy must have heard them. Through the glare, Jack saw his eyes fly open and swivel sideways, catching sight of the pair of them treading water. For a long moment Jack's eyes met Ozzy's, and then his friend's green eyelids descended again, and Jack was once more looking at a statue, granite and marble and jade mixed up together, illuminated by the brilliant beam of light that was moving closer, ever closer to that gaping hole in his crown.

Why hadn't Prince William come? No – that wasn't

right. It wasn't Prince William's fault. It was Jack's. He'd not done enough. Ozzy was about to die, Seth was about to take over – there he was now, turning his head like a great evil green pillow above the cube, laughing at Jack and Albie's misery, his face disintegrating at a spot between the two piggy eyes to allow that deathly shaft of light to penetrate.

He should have tried harder. A note under Prince William's door – what was that going to achieve? Had he dragged Prince William from his bed? Or even tried to talk to him, man to man? OK, boy to man? No, he'd gone sightseeing, for crying out loud! He, Jack Algernon Bootle-Cadogan, who'd seen enough stately homes and snooty portraits to last him a lifetime, had sauntered down the stairs looking at paintings of royal pirates with stupid earrings.

No, he was losing it now. The light shaft was tickling at the edge of the jagged space in Ozzy's skull; the wailing from Ice and her Sycamore Sisters had risen to a deafening crescendo; Albie had turned face down and was floating past him, down into the murky depths. And here Jack was, trying to work out why the piratey-looking bloke in that portrait had seemed familiar . . .

Ozzy was going. A ray of light had entered his head. And just as Seth's evil maw opened in celebration and the pool turned icy cold, Jack remembered.

28

In the gloom of death it was hard to concentrate, but Jack knew he had to focus now like he had never focused before. He desperately wanted to stop and help Albie, but there wasn't a second to spare. There wasn't a fraction of a second to spare – not even enough time to get to Minty so that she could create a few more minutes for them. The Day of Ra was upon them. His beam of light, far from ushering in the abundance in nature and goodwill for which it was intended, was being used for the ultimate destruction, and judging by the look of paralysed pain and resignation on Ozzy's face, the moment was imminent.

Far beneath the water, Jack's hand reached for his pocket. The vial, the special perfume bottle, was there, digging into his thigh. He pulled it out carefully, at the same moment picturing the glass roof above Ozzy, directly below the complacent evil head of Seth the pig. That hole . . . that hole in Seth's head . . . that was where he needed to be . . .

And suddenly he felt the wave pool shiver around him as an immense surge of power ran through him. Holding the little glass bottle high, like the Statue of Liberty's torch, Jack closed his eyes with the image of that space in Seth's forehead firmly fixed in his mind's eye. His innards seemed to fold in on themselves, and then in the next instant he was off, storming at an angle through the water, blasting Albie's floating body out of the way and managing to drive it up towards the surface at the same moment.

Zumph! Jack closed in on the foundations of the island. They passed through him like more water. *Zziiip* . . . With a peculiar ripping sound he sliced through the corner of the glass cube in which Ozzy was held, the light shaft just about to beam directly down into his open and vulnerable head. Jack's foot trailed through the high back of the throne and for a millisecond blocked the spear of light; even in water and at Zip-speed the pain was more intense and more intolerable than anything he had ever experienced in his life, and his heart swelled with compassion for what poor Ozzy must be going through.

But no more. As he surged upward the bottle cracked

through the glass pane at the top of the cube with a sound like a gunshot, directly under the open capstone, right in the path of Ra's shaft of light, straight between the eyes of the enraged pig-head.

With the stopper held firmly between his fingers, Jack stopped exactly where he had imagined himself, one foot on either side of Ozzy's head on the top of the mocking throne, his body half-in and half-out of the glass cube and his arm stretched out above his dog-head to insert the glass prism straight into the hole in Seth's face, just as he'd plant a basketball in the net.

Right as the ray of light moved directly into position.

He had to hold on to the stopper, hold on as the light seemed to pour straight down his arm and into his own heart, shielding his eyes as the glass stopper absorbed it, swelled, burst apart with iridescent shafts of light springing out in every conceivable direction, tearing apart the pulsating green face of the pig-headed god. All around him rats screamed and scrabbled out of the way but couldn't avoid the reach of the sunburst that filled the pyramid, shattered the glass, then magnified itself in every shard and splinter so that each

became a tiny sunburst of its own, like a planet exploding.

And Jack held on, quaking, in agony, waiting for
Ra to pass by so that Ozzy would be saved . . . so
that they would all be saved.

When the light turned green above his head, so bright
that it glowed through his eyelids, Jack dropped the
stopper in despair. It hadn't worked. The green light
was flowing all round him – Seth had triumphed. That
was what the noise was, the growling, ferocious roar.
Although it sounded more angry than triumphant. And
almost drowning it out was another sound . . .

Running water.

Jack opened his eyes and screamed. He appeared
to be standing at the source of an enormous fountain.
Jets of water spurted as high as the capstone – one
huge central torrent actually touched the gold of the
capstone, while the four others sprayed out in different directions. 'North, east, south and west,' he said,
mystified.

Where was it coming from? Jack looked down. His
feet were still wedged on the throne, and Ozzy was
still seated there below him, but the central water

spout appeared to be gushing directly out of Ozzy's head, straight up and past Jack's stomach, right up the pathway that the beam of light had taken. Around him the waters of the wave pool were rising rapidly, and all around the glass pyramid a series of great green shapes were taking up positions. Seth's henchmen? He couldn't see Seth, but then he couldn't see anything much with the wave pool lapping against his knees and rising fast.

But then, at the top of one of the water slides, where previously there had been only rats and the seething mass of Seth's head, he met with a peculiar sight: a red, evil eye, being tossed around on a spray of water like a kid's ball. Across the pool was another, and when he dared to look more closely Jack could see that the whole of Seth's head had been burst open by the water jets and was bobbling around on top of the various fountains. As the wave pool rose up around him, tendrils and shoots began to descend through the shattered glass of the pyramid, reaching for the water. One by one the shoots found a piece of Seth, seized it and withdrew it through the glass to fling it far into the skies. With any luck, Seth would have as much diffi-culty finding his missing bits as Ozzy his lost crown.

And talking of Ozzy . . . the throne rocked beneath Jack's feet and he found himself hanging on, then suddenly he was sailing up past the top of the water slides. To his delight, there was Albie, hanging on with his half-a-stick hooked through the rails at the top – the only way he'd stayed put when the fountain started up, Jack guessed.

'What's happening?' he yelled as Albie dropped out of sight below him.

'Osiris is growing. It's the Day of Ra!' shouted Albie. 'And the Nile will rise and the flowers bloom, and the land will be abundant and green!'

It was true. With Jack enjoying the ride with him, Ozzy on his throne had enlarged so much that he now half filled what was left of the glass pyramid, and all manner of vines and exotic flowers were tumbling down to feast on the fast-flowing waters. The green shapes beyond the glass which Jack had feared were Seth's buddies were leaning forward, smiling, waving gently through the glass. 'Sycamore Sisters!' shouted Jack. 'He's OK.'

'OK he is,' replied one of them, and Ice's enormous face appeared like the moon beside the capstone. 'Thank you, Anubis.'

Jack grinned. 'Actually, I think it's the Bootle-Cadogans you need to thank, Ice.'

He was just about to explain why when a rather shocking sound filled his canine ears. Police sirens. Fire engines. The massed forces of the Hampshire Emergency Services were on their way, by the sounds of it. Some poor neighbour must have complained that the wave pool was attracting rats, or that the pyramid appeared to have exploded.

Well, now there was something else he could do.

29

After stopping briefly in Mrs Sombourne's office, Jack met the police at the main gate beside the car park. Bone and Minty were on hand for support.

'A lot of disturbance, we were told,' said the first policeman to see them. 'Were you the ones who complained?'

'No, we, um, heard the disruption and came to help,' said Jack, concentrating hard to keep his human head on show. He stuck out his hand. 'I'm Jack Bootle-Cadogan, from Lowmount Hall.'

The policeman nodded, and then peered behind Jack. 'What's going on then?'

Actually, Jack couldn't begin to explain about the massive regeneration that was happening in and out of the pyramid. The glass would have to be replaced eventually, but Ozzy, Ice and the Sycamore Sisters were doing their best to spread the waters over the whole park so it wouldn't be flooded, and to marshal the unruly plant growth into some sort of order. There was one little problem, however, that was going to be turned to Jack's advantage.

'My father, Lord Bootle-Cadogan,' said Jack, 'sent me down here because the groundsman told him there was a rat infestation.'

'What are you, the Pied Piper?' smirked the policeman.

'Ha, no, just a . . . boy,' said Jack. 'We've got people taking care of the rats, but in the meantime there are people arriving soon who are booked in for the rest of the summer, and they need somewhere to stay.'

It would be news to Jack's parents, but he figured with a bit of Minty time-magic they could work wonders. Provided Al-Bone would agree. 'We've got thirty-two rooms up at Lowmount, suitable for small families,' he said. 'And two small cottages. One of them belonged to Bone here, but as he's going to take over the family business as the village undertaker, and write his memoirs as an archaeologist and discoverer, all paid for by my father, he's going to be too busy to be our . . . to be working up at the house much.'

Albie looked at him for a long moment, and Jack worried that he might have done the wrong thing, but then he saw him pat the pocket containing his two fob watches, and a slow smile split his face in half. It was OK. Better than OK.

'Rats,' barked one of the policewomen suddenly. 'I hate them. Better get these good people out of here,' she said.

And the ferrying of the bewildered new holiday-makers to the Lowmount Hall Holiday Home began.

Jack was ahead of the first of them by about half an hour, thanks to a bit of god-Zipping and some nifty weather patterns courtesy of Minty. Making sure he'd got his own head on, Jack skidded into the yellow drawing room where he could hear voices.

'Jack!' boomed his father as he slid along the parquet floor. 'Been looking for you.'

'Sorry,' said Jack quickly, 'but we need to get all the rooms ready, and Bone's cottage and the empty one next door. Several hundred paying guests on their way over to stay. And they all need a spa pool,' he added to his mother, who blinked and put down her teacup.

'How will we fill them all?' she whispered. 'I never

dreamed what I'd actually do with them . . .'

'Leave that to me,' said Jack. He was pretty sure Ozzy would be handy for a bit of spa-filling.

Then suddenly someone else spoke. 'It sounds as though you might have a solution to your problems, then, Jackson,' said a clear voice from the other side of the fireplace.

Jack spun round. He should have realized that his parents wouldn't just be having tea together – it would have to be in honour of a Very Important Guest. And they didn't come much more important than this one. 'Prince William,' squeaked Jack.

The prince shook his hand. 'Call me Wills. I was just passing through, thought I'd drop in and see the place. My ancestors were very fond of Lowmount – in fact, one of the Charleses stayed here on hunting trips quite regularly, I believe.'

'I believe it too,' said Jack.

It was what he'd suddenly realized when he'd been trapped next to Ozzy's body, wishing for a son of royal birth and thinking about his sightseeing trip down the stairs of Clarence House. The pirate royal in the portrait had big ear lobes – huge, worthy-of-Johnnie ear lobes. It couldn't just be a coincidence – they had to be related somehow. Somewhere in the past, a king had become involved in their ancestry, which meant that he might not be a prince, or even a lord yet, but he, Jack Bootle-Cadogan, was a son of royal blood.

'Take no notice of him, Your Highness. The boy's an idiot.' His father glared at him, then rubbed his hands together. 'Still, it sounds like we have work to do. Do you have time for a look at old Bone's cottage?'

Prince William stood up. 'Love to – it sounds fascinating. Is it haunted? Oh, nice to meet you, Jack.' And with another handshake and a friendly wink, the prince left with Jack's father.

Jack cocked his ear. 'The holidaymakers are coming, Mum. Here's the booking schedule.'

He handed her a disk pilfered from Mrs Sombourne's office, as Mr Catlow had suggested, and watched his mother's face as she headed off to the study to load it.

'It's all quite remarkable, Jack,' she said slowly. 'And now even the weather's improving. I watched the forecast earlier and it was just normal for June. Perhaps we can hang on to our past after all.'

Perhaps, thought Jack with a small, secret, wolfish smile. Perhaps they could.

Epilogue

He couldn't be back again so soon, surely? They'd only just got rid of Seth, yet Hathor scraping at Jack's window had to be a bad sign.

Jack stuck his head through the window as Hathor hovered overhead. 'Message? You'd better stick your claw in my head.'

Hathor obliged, gently, and suddenly Jack's head was filled with glorious images: a ball flying through the air; a scoreboard showing that Clearwell Comp were edging towards a draw at basketball but still needed to pull off something miraculous; and then Minty turning to face Jack, passing the ball to him . . . to him! To Jack Bootle-Cadogan, so that he could score the essential points!

It was like a dream. A cruel one at that. Maybe it *was* Seth's doing, or else what was Hathor up to? 'Is Minty in the crypt?' he demanded crossly.

Hathor let out a quiet squawk which Jack took to

mean yes, then beat his enormous wings and wheeled away.

Jack glanced back at his desk, but he'd already decided. Homework could wait. Even if this was Seth mucking everyone around, he would rather deal with that than learn about how to live off a croft in Scotland for Geography. He'd *never* have to live off a croft in Scotland. With the holidaymakers loving their stay in a stately home *with spa pool*, it looked as though the B-C family might get to stay in Lowmount Hall with happy staff and customers for a good many years. Taking a second to morph into Doghead, Jack hurled himself out of the window and Zipped across to the crypt.

So no one could surprise him, Jack pictured the inside of Granny Dazzle's sarcophagus, Zipped to it invisibly, then popped his head up on top of the tomb.

Albie's shiny shoes were on a level with his nose. 'Very unconventional,' said Albie, putting down his fighting stick.

'That's gross,' said Minty. 'Can't you just turn up like a normal god?'

'A normal god,' repeated Jack. 'I'm not sure what

that means. And what was all that about? Clearwell Comp's basketball crisis and you passing me the ball. You're just rubbing it in, aren't you? Honestly, I feel bad enough about being kicked off the team.'

Minty and Albie shared a secretive grin. 'I know. I was feeling a bit bad about it too. But I reckon that we can persuade Fraser to let you back on the team, provided you can control yourself, and provided you've learned how to play . . . how to *really* play.'

'Is this one of your weird unfunny jokes?' said Jack. 'How am I going to learn to "really" play without a team to practise with?'

Minty stuck out a hand. 'Sorry, you are going to have to hold it,' she said gruffly, 'but you'll thank me for it later.'

'Do what she says, Jack,' said Albie. 'Remember, I am the one who knows everything.'

'What's going on?'

'The game of basketball is going on right now, in fact,' said Albie, jumping down from the sarcophagus and holding up the radio. 'Ozzy'n'Ice have sneaked in with the transmitter of the waves and are sending the results. It's close to the end. Your school is going to lose.'

Jack looked around, bewildered. 'Well, thanks. Nice of you to tell me.'

Grabbing his hand roughly, Minty tutted. 'Don't you remember anything? We are gods, OK? I can turn back time, Ice can freeze the substitution bench and then you can win the game and Fraser will let you back on the team.'

'But I'm hopeless.'

Minty rolled her eyes. 'Hathor's creating a cloud, gives us about ten earth minutes. So Zip us. You and me. Now.'

'What's going on?' Jack stared at them both. 'Zip where?'

'The *ball*room,' said Minty and Albie together.

Albie grinned. 'Go ahead. I'll get to see it all one day.'

And suddenly Jack realized what they both meant. The ballroom which could house a thousand ballrooms, which accommodated a thousand spirits, was not just a place to dance, to greet people. It was a place where ball games – great, godly ball games – could be played.

Furthermore, he, Jack Algernon Anubis Bootle-Cadogan, was just the one to get them there, and he didn't have to be dead to do it. He gripped Minty's wrist tightly, closed his eyes, and pictured the enormous room. The twist in his gut was monumental, but he kept his eyes shut tight and his mind on that one image, without wavering.

And when he opened them again, the sides were all in position – the Waites and Percy and Mrs Percy and several other people from the graveyard, and his own family, Granny Dazzle and Lord Jay and Johnnie with the Ear Lobes; and opposing them, ready to play, an energetic Mr Catlow and his old rugby team.

Jack stared for a long moment, then whispered to Minty, 'This is all very well, but I thought you said we'd be playing with gods . . .'

'You're a god, I'm a god,' said Minty, 'and you'd be amazed who else could turn out to be gods in the end.'

'Well, if you're sure,' said Jack uncertainly, looking at the assembled ghosts. It didn't seem likely that any of them would be morphing into gods any time soon. But then, as he'd discovered, god-status could be bestowed on the most unlikely people. And this lot certainly all appeared to be ready for a good go at basketball.

'Pick your side, Jack,' called Mr Catlow with a smile. 'It's a new game for us, but I think we'll be pretty handy.'

'I'm with you then,' said Minty, and she sniffed as she strode past Jack. 'Ready, Doghead?'

'Sure am, Hawkhead,' he replied. He high-fived Lord Jay, hugged his great-grandmother and poised himself ready to play. Focus. He just had to concentrate.

This was going to be fun.

Find out how it all began . . .

Jane Blonde

'Until now, you have been just plain old Janey Brown. But you are going to grow and grow. You will be what your parents have not allowed you to be. It's in your past. And it's in your future. There's a whole new part of you just waiting to burst out. You are Jane Blonde – Sensational Spylet. Welcome to our world.'

Follow Jane Blonde on her first non-stop mission!

Jane Blonde

spies trouble

Jane's purr-ecious spy-cat, Trouble, has been kidnapped! A group of mad scientists think they have discovered the secret to a cat's nine lives – but they need Trouble for their experiments. All the clues lead down the drain – spying can be a wet and stinky business! But with chewing gum that lets her breathe underwater, a SPIpod tracking device and a high-speed mini-hoverboard, Jane Blonde is ready for ACTION . . .

Jane Blonde
twice the spylet

Jane Blonde, Sensational Spylet, has just met her secret twin!

When the sisters are posted to an Australian sheep farm, Janey's instincts are on red alert. There's something weird about those sheep. Come to think of it, there's something suspicious about Jane Blonde's twin . . .

Janey can raise an invisible shield with her spy-ring and she can burrow through the earth with her spy-drill boots – but will incredible gadgets save her this time?

A selected list of titles available from Macmillan Children's Books

The prices shown below are correct at the time of going to press. However, Macmillan Publishers reserves the right to show new retail prices on covers, which may differ from those previously advertised.

Jill Marshall

Doghead	978-0-330-45153-6	£5.99
Jane Blonde, Sensational Spylet	978-0-330-43814-8	£5.99
Jane Blonde Spies Trouble	978-0-330-43825-4	£5.99
Jane Blonde, Twice the Spylet	978-0-330-44657-0	£5.99
Jane Blonde, Spylet on Ice	978-0-330-44658-7	£5.99
Jane Blonde, Goldenspy	978-0-230-53244-1	£5.99
Jane Blonde, Spy in the Sky	978-0-330-45812-2	£5.99
Jane Blonde, Spylets Are Forever	978-0-330-45813-9	£5.99

All Pan Macmillan titles can be ordered from our website, www.panmacmillan.com, or from your local bookshop and are also available by post from:

Bookpost, PO Box 29, Douglas, Isle of Man IM99 1BQ
Credit cards accepted. For details:
Telephone: 01624 677237
Fax: 01624 670923
Email: bookshop@enterprise.net
www.bookpost.co.uk

Free postage and packing in the United Kingdom